The Garbage Man's Daughter

Book 1

Letting Go of Shame

GLORIA SHELL MITCHELL

Eb
EncourageMint Books
Inglewood, CA

ISBN: **978-0-9761010-0-0**
Library of Congress Control Number: 2010939770

THE GARBAGE MAN'S DAUGHTER Series by Gloria Shell Mitchell is a work of creative nonfiction. The names have been changed to protect the identities of the innocent, or otherwise.

Scripture quotations are taken from the *Holy Bible,* New Living Translation, copyright © 1996. Used by permission of Tyndale House Publishers, Inc., Wheaton, Illinois 60189. All rights reserved.

Published by:

Eb

EncourageMint Books
P.O. Box 5596
Inglewood, CA 90310-5596
www.encouragemintbooks.com

Cover Design by: kadesigns1@aol.com
Page Layout by: nosyrosydesigns@gmail.com

Printed in the United States
Email: gloriashellmitchell@gmail.com

DEDICATION

THE GARBAGE MAN'S DAUGHTER series is dedicated to all the people who inspired me to write.

I dedicate this book series in loving memory to my beloved parents, James "Jasper" Shell and Minnie Pelzer Shell, my grandparents, Jervia Pelzer, Carrie Gantt Pelzer, and Jake Shell, my sisters Carrie June, Marie Harmon, Diane Purvis, and Melba Shell, my brother Alexander Shell and nephew Alphonso Shell, my cousin Benjamin F. Pelzer, Jr., my aunt Rose Ann Shuler and her daughter, Maggie Dozier whose impact upon my life are included.

I give special mother recognition to my daughters, Richette Bell and Joy Christin Mitchell who know the pain of children of divorce, and to alumni of my divorce support groups *Prayerfully Addressing Divorce* and *Laugh, Love and Live Again.*

I dedicate this work to the following precious individuals: my brother James and sisters Elizabeth, Mattie, MeLinda, Deborah, Josephine, Gwendolyn, Bessie, Cynthia; my Uncle Benjamin Pelzer and Aunt Willie Mae Pelzer; unmarried mothers and absentee fathers; school teachers; and all who are sick, hurting, abused, neglected, rejected, and confused.

SPECIAL THANKS
and
ACKNOWLEDGEMENTS

I AM DEEPLY INDEBTED to my writing coach and editor, Martha Tucker of Premiere Writers, who took me by the hand and walked me across the finish line with the manuscript that I began writing in 1985. I offer special thanks to my online writing group members, Yolantha Harrison-Pace, Janice Lauderdale and Dena McLemore.

Johnny Morris, my program engineer at radio station KTYM in Inglewood, CA encouraged me to finish this project so he could record my audio book.

My accountability partners, Kenneth Franklin and Barbara Lindsey, listened and elaborated on each chapter read in our Christian Teachers Association dinner meetings.

My prayer partner since 1988, Emma Richardson, age 93, insisted that I read the entire manuscript to her. Prayer partners Beverly Williams and Lillian Laffitte, the clergy in The Gathering of Reverend Sisters Fellowship led by Rev. Barbara Jean Jenkins, and members of my church family at Faithful Central Bible Church in Inglewood, CA provided much needed prayer support.

Manuscript readers, English teachers Addie Burroughs and Laurel Simpson, as well as author, Victoria Wilson Darrah, provided honest feedback.

My friends, Linda Nisby Johnson, Christine Parham, Brenda Darby, Darlene Colbert, Frizell Randolph Smith, Valerie Elston, and others read and offered suggestions for improvement.

I gained ideas for improvement from authors Richard Krawiec, Candace Cole, Sha' Givens, Rosie Milligan, Sharon Norris Elliott, Vivica Keyes and editors Joyce Martin, Gwen Pierre, and Nichole Palmer.

My Lord and Savior, Jesus Christ, showed me the life issues to be addressed in this book series and convinced me that there are "no things" that happen by coincidence. I learned that God uses every experience to teach us life lessons.

Finally, I express my sincere gratitude to the teachers at C.A. Johnson High School during the 1960s, all past, present and future public and private school teachers and other educators. Thank you for your commitment to teach succeeding generations.

FOREWORD

Into the furnace let me go alone;
Stay you without in terror of the heat.
I will go naked in–for thus 'tis sweet–
into the weird depths of the hottest zone.

AN EXCERPT FROM *BAPTISM* BY CLAUDE MCKAY
SELECTED POEMS (1953)

THIS FIRST BOOK written by my sister, The Reverend Dr. Gloria Shell Mitchell, is very much a baptism by fire. She walks boldly where few of us dare to go, writing an intimate portrayal of a family with all of its warts, foibles, and secrets.

I am honored to be given the opportunity to write the foreword to Gloria's book "The Garbage Man's Daughter." I marvel that after months of editing and revisions I am able to say, my sister has written a book!

The Book is provocative; part memoir, part Greek tragedy, it has hurt and humor in each chapter. It tells everyone that although you may be born into a life that seems destitute and destined for failure, there is a way out. This is truly what my sister has always lived and believed. Gloria came up from poverty but turned around and threw down a rope, many times, to help others up.

Sis: I'm very proud of your achievement, birthing this baby! Now, you no longer have to hear the annoying question, "how is the book coming?"

Elizabeth Shell Carr, LCSW
Writer, psychotherapist
Brooklyn, NY

Introduction

"This above all: to thine own self be true,
And it must follow, as the night the day,
Thou canst not then be false to any man."

A QUOTE BY LORD POLONIUS IN ACT 1. SCENE III
OF *HAMLET* BY WILLIAM SHAKESPEARE

I HAD A LIFELONG HABIT OF DOODLING wherever I was until the day someone asked, "What are you always writing?" That's when I realized that I always scribbled *BOOK*. Once I decided to write a book, my doodling habit vanished.

I have noticed that people often suppress, rather than openly address, negative childhood experiences. Consequently, facades are worn, pleasant and superficial topics are freely discussed, and shallow relationships are formed. By facilitating divorce recovery groups, I clearly observed that shame hinders healing and even promotes sickness. Past hurts, no matter how shameful, must be recognized and dumped like garbage for wounded people to stop hurting others and themselves.

While recovering from my own divorce, I often asked, "Why me, Lord?" Eventually, God replied, "Why not you? When I strengthen you, go strengthen your sisters and brothers."

Therefore, *The Garbage Man's Daughter* series was written to strengthen and promote inner healing in readers who know the pain and shame of brokenness, especially family dysfunction and divorce. Davida Kincaid, who represents me and nameless others, simplistically shares her painful journey toward love, acceptance, wholeness and genuine relationships.

May you remember the famous Shakespearean quote, "to thine own self be true" as you ponder the reflection questions in the back of the book.

CHAPTER 1

"AW-SHUCKS, NOT HIM AGAIN!" I mumbled as I stepped into our tiny cluttered living room. It was only our second Friday night in the country when I laid eyes on Mama's bald-headed boyfriend, Mr. Fred, from Marshall Village. He didn't even give us time to get used to our new house out here in the woods before he showed up last Friday night.

Mr. Fred stood toe-to-toe in front of Mama like a skinny tree swaying in the wind. His shiny bald peanut head bobbed a wee bit above Mama's five-foot chocolate frame. Her tiny hands gripped his waist to keep him from falling.

Let him fall! I thought. A good bump on his head might knock some sense into him. I chuckled and stepped up my pace. He turned his head and looked at me as I stomped past them. I'm sure he noticed that this nine-year-old girl didn't like him one bit. When I rolled my eyes like I was slicing him with a knife, he knew better than to say a word to me. I hated seeing him in my mama's face like that. There was no way he could ever take my daddy's place. NEVER! NEVER! NEVER!

The puckered linoleum rug squeaked real loud as I crossed the floor. I wanted to startle the two lovebirds. In my head, the floor screamed, "Go home! Go home!" to the rhythm of my footsteps. I rather enjoyed the rhythm because the words clearly expressed how I felt. I brushed past Mr. Fred and Mama as I headed for the kitchen. Playing kickball outside in the June heat had made me thirsty. I wished I could kick him out of our house but I knew that pretty soon he and Mama would disappear into her bedroom. In a way, that was good because I couldn't stand to see them together.

I was tired of that man stealing my mama from us. It was bad enough that he stole her from Daddy. Ever since we moved, we never see much of her until after Mr. Fred is gone.

I placed the old beat up metal bucket full of water I had just drawn from the well on the kitchen table and muttered softly, "Seeing that sloppy drunk all weekend is just as bad as taking a dose of Cod Liver Oil. Both of them leave a bad taste in my mouth and make me want to puke. Ugh!" I made an ugly face and smiled at my thoughts.

I imagined myself thumping Mr. Fred on the head as I scooped eight dippers of water and poured them in the half-gallon plastic pitcher. I picked a pack of cherry Kool-Aid from a sealed plastic container on the table, thumped it a couple of times to loosen the powder, ripped open the pack at one corner, and emptied the bag into the water. I stirred in two cups of Dixie Crystals granulated sugar that I took from the five-pound bag in the airtight grocery can. I could imagine Mr. Fred's head throbbing from a thump on his head.

I don't know how Mama with her pretty teeth can stand to look at that man's snaggleteeth and smell his whiskey breath. I can't stand the way he brags about being good at everything but never shows anything he's done. My Uncle Clyde says, "That man can't even hold his liquor!"

I stirred the drink with a long silver spoon and tasted a little bit on the tip of my tongue. "Ummm. Needs a little more sugar," I said to myself. I dumped in a tad more sugar straight from the bag then turned to the refrigerator for a lemon in the vegetable bin. Wouldn't you know? No lemons.

I wish I could go, one... two... three... and poof! Mr. Fred would disappear. I smiled at how silly that sounded. Last week I wished Mr. Fred would disappear and never come back. Well, he showed up the same time this Friday night. It seems to me that he'd be able to see that our little country house is full of children and there's no room for him. I'll bet his mama's glad to get rid of him when he comes out here on Friday night.

"C'mon Sunday night and take what Uncle Clyde calls 'this poor excuse of a man' out of our house," I cried softly.

I dumped a whole tray of ice cubes in the red liquid and poured myself a full glass. Then I snatched open the café curtains so I could see what was happening in the living room. I saw Mr. Fred stagger backward while Mama held on to him until he plopped down on the sofa. The moment the springs squeaked on my bed I yelled at him, "Get off my bed! I don't want to smell your pee like I did last week. Mama, make him get up!"

"I'll take care of him!" Mama yelled back. "You just mind your own business!" She yanked Mr. Fred's arms and practically pulled him off the sofa bed. She flung his right arm over her shoulder and guided him to her bedroom.

"Yep! There they go!" I said as I let go of the kitchen curtain.

I heard the mattress squeal as Mr. Fred fell on it with the thud of a chopped down tree. "If only he'll just stay in the bedroom until it's time for him to leave on Sunday night," I mumbled. I closed my eyes, crossed my middle and index fingers, and made a wish. "Stay in there!"

I liked it better when we lived in Marshall Village and Mama went up to Mr. Fred's apartment while Daddy was in the hospital. But now that Daddy's gone and we've moved to this country house, Mr. Fred pays somebody to bring his drunk self to visit Mama. Daddy never got sloppy drunk and peed on himself, but this man falls down, vomits, and staggers around all the time.

It's downright disgusting the way he likes to hug everybody and slobber on us. He talks so much he foams at the mouth like a mad dog. I'm glad he knew I meant what I said when I screamed at him, "If you ever touch me again I'll hurt you!" Even if I am nine I gave him a piece of my mind 'cause he deserved it.

I drank the tall glass of cherry Kool-Aid then poured another half glass. While staring at droplets rolling down outside my glass of cold drink, I said, "I can't figure out what Mama sees in him anymore than I can figure out how water drops got on the outside of this glass."

The drink was a pretty red color and it smelled and tasted good too. But Mr. Fred? I shook my head. Oh yeah, I guess Mama puts up with him for the twenty dollars he gives her every Friday night. I wondered how he lived off whiskey most of the time. Having him at our house made no sense. If Mama just wanted a man, she could have stayed with Daddy.

I gulped the last of my drink, rinsed out the glass and put it in the dishpan. Here I am drinking a five-cent pack of Kool-Aid that has to be shared with my whole family while that man has money to spend on Jack Daniels whiskey, I thought. I just don't understand it. I headed back outdoors wondering how anybody could pay more for something to drink than for food to eat.

* * *

Later that night, I pulled the sofa away from the wall and pushed on the back to turn it into my bed. I was thinking, if only Mama knew how hard it is to fall asleep when my nostrils have to smell Mr. Fred's pee! As if the smell of his old pee wasn't bad enough, I told her that bedbugs crawl on me as soon as I get comfortable. I fight the little critters as long as I'm awake but I can't stay awake all night. I tucked a sheet in the cracks of the sofa and laid my pillow on one end. I tied a scarf tight around my head to keep bedbugs from crawling in my ears. I sighed when my bed was made. I knew if I managed to fall asleep, I could at least get a little rest before the bedbugs attacked.

"Bedtime!" I shouted. My brother Harry and little sisters Vera, April and Gladys came running over to me. I glanced over at Mama's closed bedroom door. "Oh well!" I sighed again.

We joined hands in a circle to recite our nightly prayer together: "Goodnight. Sleep tight. Don't let the bedbugs bite. Do what's right, with all your might. Goodnight."

After they marched off to bed, I turned off the light and knelt down to say my private prayer, "Lord, please let me be able to go to sleep. Amen."

I settled down between a sheet folded lengthwise and drifted off to sleep almost as soon as my head hit the pillow. It wasn't long before I jumped up and ran across the room and flicked on the light. Thousands of those little bloodsuckers ran every which way. I was so mad at them.

I had sprayed the cracks and corners of that green pleather chair what seemed like a thousand times, but those bedbugs kept on attacking me. I took revenge and smashed hundreds of them with my hand. They must have seen me closing in on them as I smashed more and more of them. But when I realized that the fresh blood oozing from their bodies onto my hand was mine, I no longer felt victorious. When I was worn out from fighting bedbugs, I wiped my hands on the washcloth I kept beside my pillow and lay back down. I left the light on, hoping they would be too afraid to come back. I stretched out on my back with my eyes wide open and waited for sleep to come. What had I done to have to live like this?

I thought about the day that seemed so long ago when Mama walked in from work, saying, "My brother's coming tomorrow to move us to the country."

I was so shocked I couldn't say a word. Somebody please tell me why I had to give up my comfortable bed in Marshall Village, in the city, to move to this dreadful place in the woods outside Columbia?

Thoughts and more thoughts flooded my mind as I lay there in the dimness staring at the ceiling light. I kept thinking back to that day when my whole life changed.

CHAPTER 2

I LAY IN BED THINKING back to the day we moved from Marshall Village to the country. Our move had been sudden, and to me, unnecessary. Just like Mama said, Uncle Clyde backed his red pickup in front of our Marshall Village apartment on Saturday morning, the day after I finished third grade. He and his helper, dressed in white tee shirts and blue jeans like a set of twins, stomped inside our apartment and started taking beds apart and moving furniture out of the house and hauling it away. After all the furniture was gone, my brother and sisters and I were sitting on the truck bed the last time Uncle Clyde drove away.

My sister Beverly looked over at me and said, "Life in the country is going to be a hair-raising experience." She laughed.

I laughed too because I saw how hard she was trying to keep the wind from blowing her hair in her eyes. As I lay in my bedbug-infested bed thinking about that day, I can honestly say I'm not laughing now because what she said was true.

The very first day in the country was sizzling hot. I felt like I'd walked into an oven as I struggled with a bag of clothes, dragging it into our new square blockhouse. I took one look around our tiny bedroom and right then I knew I was going to hate living out here.

"I want to go back to Marshall Village where we left my daddy, my oldest sister, all my friends, my school, my church, my godparents, and Cooper's corner store," I begged. "I want to go back home!"

I don't know why I complained to my brother Harry, but I did. I guess I always turned to him because he listened to me, even though he usually didn't say much to anybody.

"People are supposed to move to better houses like we did when we moved from the duplex downtown to Marshall Village," I grumbled. "Naw, not us! We moved to this two-bedroom house made out of ugly, gray concrete blocks. We only got a living room, kitchen, and two bedrooms on six acres of nothing but trees. You know a house should be bigger than this."

Harry started to go out of the room, but I pulled his shirttail. "Whoever heard of a house with no bathroom in it? I'm not going down some slippery clay path to use that stink outhouse full of flies and spider webs. You can't even have privacy with all those big cracks in that rotten, pine wood with knots in it."

"Well, – " Harry shrugged his shoulders but didn't try to leave.

"When we first got here I had to use it. A big bumblebee flew in there and I tried to swat it with a paper sack. I ended up ripping my tank top on a rusty nail that was sticking through the wood when I tried to open the door so I could get out in a hurry. Look at my top."

"Sis, I saw Mama put a pot behind her bed."

"There ought to be a law against outdoor toilets. It's scary to go in that little house. It's too stink to breathe in there. And peeing in a little pot in the house is crazy!"

"Well, sis, you could—"

"We could go back to Marshall Village that's what."

"I hear you Sis," Harry said.

"Well, I guess if we have a choice, the night pot won't be so bad after all!" I rattled on. "Why would anybody build a house and put the bathroom outdoors? That's my ten thousand dollar question that I hope somebody will answer for me one day 'cause it makes absolutely no sense to me now!" I stood in the middle of the kitchen floor with my arms folded, breathing hard at Harry who was sitting on his bed in a corner of the kitchen. I shook my head in disgust and took a long, deep breath.

"The only good thing about the move to the country is living next door to Grandpa and Grandma Cox," I said. "It feels good being able to go over there and always find the door unlocked. It seems like I have two houses rather than one, especially when it rains. I just love wading in the water that flows down the hill from our house. It makes a little rushing river around their front porch that seems to say, "Come on in, the water's fine."

When I turned my head while making gestures to describe the rushing water, Harry jumped up and sneaked toward the backdoor.

"Why didn't you just tell me to hush?" I yelled as he ran out the door. "Oh well, thanks anyhow for listening as long as you did."

I walked over to the kitchen door and looked at all the pine trees behind our house and Grandpa's. I remembered standing on the hill facing the woods and counting treetops the day we moved to the country and Grandpa Cox – looking like a tree himself – interrupted my count.

"We got mostly Pines," he said.

I gave up counting because Pines were everywhere.

"Looks like Johnny Appleseed camped here for years and planted Pine trees every day," I told Grandpa. "Children are supposed to have a yard to play in, like we had in Marshall Village, not trees everywhere."

"Trees help ya breathe fresh air," he said.

"The only yard we have to play in is the dirt driveway between the two houses," I complained. "I sure am glad the shortcut through the vegetable garden is not scary like Creepy Crater was in Marshall Village." I pointed to a thorn bush loaded with red roses in the corner of the garden.

"Those roses smell good, except when you spread cow manure," I told Grandpa.

"Your grandma and I like living out here in da woods," Grandpa said. "Nobody bothers us."

By harvest time, Grandpa sure had done a lot. He'd put up a wire fence to keep people and animal feet away from the neatly plowed rows of cabbage, okra, string beans, tomatoes, strawberries, collards, corn, sugar cane, and watermelons in his garden. When the fence went up, we knew it was time to go in the garden and fight those big prickly tomato worms. The sight of those worms convinced me that taking the long way around the garden was not a bad idea.

When Mama walked into the kitchen that night wearing a tight skirt that showed her big behind and tiny waist, I began blurting out.

"Mama, how did we end up living in the house your oldest brother built for himself?" I asked as she stared at the square hunk of cornbread I was eating. I secretly wished Uncle Ezekiel would come home and kick us out so we could move back to Marshall Village.

"We moved in this empty house because we needed a place to stay after my husband left," Mama said. This house has been empty ever since my brothers Ezekiel and Moses walked all the way to downtown Columbia and joined the Army. And after they enlisted, my three younger brothers, Clyde, Cupid and Daniel tried to enlist too. The Army rejected Cupid and Daniel 'cause they were too young but they turned Clyde down flat 'cause he had asthma. My brothers were determined to get away from my mama so they didn't take 'no' for an answer. Three weeks later Cupid and Daniel hitchhiked all the way to Charleston where they lied about their age and enlisted in the Army too. That left only my brother Clyde and me at home."

"I don't blame them for running away from the country," I said. "There's too much work to do around this place."

Mama paid no attention to me. "I reckon Clyde, with that fat belly of his was too lazy to work. He hated being left behind. That's probably why he married Judy and moved to Marshall Village," she said.

"Now his fat belly is still enjoying living in Marshall Village while we're out here in this country fighting creepy critters and working hard just to have food to eat," I said under my breath.

And oh, I almost forgot, I said to myself, I have to put up with Mr. Fred while wishing for my daddy.

This was my last thought before I yawned and drifted off to sleep.

* * *

I woke up early Saturday morning to the sound of a rooster crowing. I was ready for a new lesson from Grandpa Cox. I ran next door and found him taking a square white cardboard box out of the freezer. When he laid it on the table I read the box top.

"What are chit-ter-lings?" I asked Grandpa.

"Baby, you didn't say dat right," he said. "Them's chitlins and they's good eatin."

"Then why does it say, "Chit-ter-lings" on the box?" I asked. I was confused.

"That's cause whoever wrote that word never had none," Grandpa replied. He laughed at his own joke.

I laughed too. I loved Grandpa Cox because he spent lots of time teaching me. I followed him outside to the barn where he gave hands-on lessons about country living. "S-l-i-d-e yo hand 'neath da hen to git da eggs like dis here," he said while showing me his sliding hand. It sounded easy enough, so I leaned over and gently slid my hand beneath the hen and removed a smooth oval egg from a little pile of hay. The hen went, "cluck, cluck, cluck."

"The same to you," I whispered. I felt guilty–like a thief stealing chicks to kill and eat for dinner. Suddenly I cried, "Ouch!" when the hen pecked my naked skin and it hurt. I jerked my hand away, dropping the egg and rubbing my pain. "That hurt!" I cried.

Grandpa reached down and snatched up the hen that pecked my hand. The hen had laid six fresh eggs inside a pile of hay. I guess she was sitting on them to hide them.

"Ya gotta act like ya know whatcha doing so they kin trust ya," he said.

"Oh, now you tell me," I pouted.

After a few more pecks, I started acting like I knew what I was doing while stealing hen eggs. But I kept my distance from that cocky rooster that strutted around like he owned the whole barnyard. He had an evil look in his eyes.

"Take them eggs to your grandma," Grandpa said. "Go slow so ya won't crack 'em."

I carefully held the Easter basket containing a dozen fresh eggs by the handle as I took baby steps down the hill to Grandma's house. I watched the eggs every step of the way to make sure they didn't roll around. I walked inside and gently placed the basket on the kitchen table.

"Fresh eggs, Grandma!" I hollered.

Grandma turned away from the kitchen stove and picked up one egg in each hand. She glanced at all the eggs in the basket.

"I see Jerry's got ya working. Ya done good, child."

"Thanks, Grandma!" I shouted and ran back toward the door. I spotted Grandpa wearing brown overalls closing the wooden gate to the fenced yard where Old Bessie was standing quietly in one spot. I ran over to the yard and crawled through the wooden posts in the fence so I could get to Grandpa. I watched him sit down on a three-legged stool with a milk bucket in his hand. He yanked Old Bessie's tits and her milk made a strange noise as it squirted into the empty bucket. The more he squirted, the less noise the milk made. Grandpa yanked a couple of tits until no more milk came out.

"Wanna try it now?" Grandpa asked.

"Yes Sir," I said.

He patted Old Bessie's fat belly and removed his hand. "Here, put yo hand on her tit like dis," he said as he took my hand and placed it on one tit.

I got tickled as I wrapped my hand around Old Bessie's tit. I giggled and Bessie turned her head toward me and went, "M-o-o." I pulled the tit but no milk came out.

"Ya gotta show her ya da boss," he said. "Act like ya know what ya doing when ya pull the cow's tit."

The next time I pulled hard on the tit and milk squirted up in my face rather than down in the bucket. I giggled as I wiped fresh milk from my eyes. Grandpa laughed heartily as he pushed the bucket into the right spot.

"Try it 'gain," he said.

I guess I did it right because Old Bessie didn't move or moo, and milk squirted into the bucket. I felt like I was robbing the cow of milk for her calf, even though she didn't have one. From that day on I had fun milking Old Bessie.

It was fascinating to watch Grandpa kill a chicken. Sometimes he grabbed it by the feet and chopped off the head with a hatchet. I couldn't figure out how a chicken with no head could run around in circles until it dropped dead, but it was still amazing to watch. Other times he would wring the chicken's neck and drop the animal on the ground so it could run around flapping its wings until it finished dying. Yucky, yuk, yuk! I felt sorry for innocent chickens that fought hard to stay alive when they were already dead. And I could not even force myself to eat a chicken that I saw Grandpa kill.

"I think killing harmless chickens is animal cruelty," I told Grandpa.

"Why do ya think the good Lawd made dese birds so tasty?" he asked. "Jes so they kin run 'round the yard 'til they die?"

"Well, you're right again," I said. Grandpa's answers made a whole lot of sense.

After the chicken dropped dead, Grandpa dipped it in a big pot of boiling hot water and handed me a wet bird by its feet.

"Pluck off da feathers like dis," he said. He pulled big feathers out of the chicken's body and they slid right out. I was surprised to see how easy it was to pluck the feathers.

"What did you do with the chicken feet?" I asked while plucking the chicken.

"Well, I chopped 'em off, cut off the toenails with scissors, and they's in the pot boiling rat now. I'll fetch one fo ya after while." Grandpa went inside and soon returned with a chicken foot. He peeled the skin off the foot like he was peeling an orange and I got another surprise. When boiled and seasoned, the meaty part of bony chicken feet taste good.

"Chicken feet taste good, Grandpa," I said. "I sure am glad you cut off those yellow fingernails or toenails, whichever they are."

"Foots got toenails," he said.

In no time at all, Grandpa showed me how to do a lot of other things in the busy farmyard. I tied sticks into a bundle to make a broom to sweep the driveway and yard, used an ax to chop down trees and split logs for firewood, primed a pump to get running water in my grandparents' house, tossed a bucket in a well and drew water with a rope, and untangled the clothes that wrapped around the wringer of his washing machine. I dug white potatoes out of the ground, parched peanuts in a brick hearth, canned watermelon rind and other peelings that we used to throw in the garbage before we moved to the country, and shook pecans off the tree rather than wait for the husks to open so the nuts could fall to the ground.

Dang! There's a big difference in living in the country from living in the city.

* * *

It was hard to believe that one Saturday morning I stretched out in a bathtub half full of hot and cold running water in Marshall Village, and the next morning I realized that not everybody can take a hot bath.

In my new country home, there was no water but well water, no faucet, no bathtub, and no bathroom in the house. Besides struggling to bathe while standing up in a round tin tub, I struggled to learn how to wash wet clothes on a glass scrub board without getting blisters on my hands. I must admit that it was kind of fun folding sheets taken off the clothesline. Folding sheets was kind of like dancing with a partner. You have to start off right to end up right.

It took me awhile to learn how to neatly stack firewood without causing an avalanche. Many times I had to restack the woodpile behind the kitchen stove because I pulled the wrong log. And Mama had the nerve to fuss at me when I used too much kindling to start a fire.

"Heck, I don't know what I'm doing," I murmured to myself.

My palms turned red from rubbing newspaper or brown paper bags to make soft toilet tissue. Sometimes I made a mess while I was learning how to pee in a night pot without sitting down on it. I think my greatest challenge was sitting on the outdoor toilet without looking at the crap below the seat. Prayer is definitely in order when your private parts are vulnerable to a bee string, a fly or something worse.

Grandpa gave me lots of safety tips about how to handle matches. When we were out of kindling, I learned how to make a fire with rolled up newspaper without snuffing out the flame. I also learned how to pour the right amount of kerosene on firewood, lift a twenty-pound sack of coals without injuring my back, get up extra early to make a fire to heat up the cast iron stove, heat water for bathing, wash up using a wash basin, recognize when heat from the fireplace had parched my legs even when my backside was freezing cold, be on time to catch the school bus, and adjust to walking through chicken and goose poop sprinkled all over the yard.

I couldn't understand why Daddy never came to visit us and Mr. Fred came every Friday. Every time I thought about life in Marshall Village I told Mama, "I miss my daddy." I liked saying that when Mr. Fred came to visit.

I could count on Mama saying, "You'll get over it."

I felt like somebody needed to remind her she was still a married woman. When Mama's boyfriend came to our house I felt like running away and hiding until he left. But there was no place to hide in the scary country woods.

My grandpa had made sure to tell me how dangerous it was out among the trees.

"Something or somebody could snatch ya out in them woods!" he warned us.

I got knots in my stomach just thinking about how far I had to walk out in the country to get to the nearest store. That was no fun.

"Why did Mama bring us out here?" was a question I wished somebody could answer for me as random thoughts scrambled my brain.

Instead of seeing children playing outdoors like we did in Marshall Village, all I ever saw were dogs, cats, cows, chickens and other animals everywhere, pooping before my very eyes. It was annoying to have to inhale the mingled odors from fertilizer, animals, outdoor toilets, slop, roses and other crap.

"Did anybody ask us if we wanted to move out here?" I blurted. I wanted Mama to hear me complaining to Harry.

Harry just stared at me with a blank face and big round eyes.

He's no help, but at least he listens, I thought. It was hard to believe that nobody else in my family complained but me. Country living was a totally different way of life for all of us. I had to learn new vocabulary words like, "cow teats" instead of "tits" according to my big sister Beverly who loved to use big words," new foods, new animals, new people, and new information necessary for survival.

"Ya gotta learn dis or you kin get yoself hurt," Grandpa constantly warned me. "Vida, ya da eldest, ya gotta teach da younger chillen."

Since I had to teach others, I tried to make learning fun. I quickly learned how to eat and drink foods I had never heard of before, strange sounding things like liver pudding, pig feet, pig ears, buttermilk, hog head cheese, tripe, chicken feet, hickory nuts, and goose eggs. I picked only ripe strawberries, no green ones. I guarded my hands from the green tomato worms, which really are scary-looking caterpillars. And I carefully avoided bruising the skin when digging up the white and sweet potatoes. With Grandpa's guidance I learned how to use the ax, hoe, pick, hedge clippers, sling blade and wheel barrow almost as well as he could.

"Show me ya muscles," Grandpa said one day after I finished clipping the hedges in front of his house.

I clenched my fist and raised my right arm to show him my bulging bicep. I smiled proudly when he pressed the hard bulge.

"Keep on working, he said. Child, ya coming 'long jes fine," he said.

Occasionally Grandma showed me how to do women's work. As if all Grandpa's lessons weren't enough to learn, Grandma taught me things like how to protect clothes hanging on the wall from soot by hanging them in plastic dry cleaning bags tied at the top and bottom. She showed me how to cover the mattress with hard plastic beneath the sheet to protect it from yellow stains when somebody peed in the bed. When my old black and white saddle oxfords got holes in them, my grandma showed me how to carefully measure, cut a piece of cardboard box and put it in my shoe so nobody would know I had holes in my soles. She let me sort dried beans and put them in a big pot of water to cook for hours. The longer they cooked, the less water was in the pot. It's interesting that the beans looked like little rocks before they were cooked but afterward they were tender, juicy and yummy for the tummy.

"Out here, we have to make our own fun since the nearest neighbors with children are a quarter mile away," I told Harry.

"Not me," Harry said. "I got friends up the road." He walked on outside like he didn't even miss playing with the children in Marshall Village.

After he left, I thought about the first week we moved in the country. Everybody on Cashmere Road got up at dawn to go pick blackberries off the vines before the snakes got to them. That was fun for me because people of all ages showed up with jars, cups and buckets and parted the bushes in search of ripe berries.

I was glad they told my little sisters and me to wear long pants to keep the briars from scratching our legs. After we had picked all the blackberries off the vines on the ground, I looked up and spotted some on a huge tree deep in the woods.

"What about the berries on that tree over there?" I asked, pointing to some plump berries.

"Hey, hey, hey!" shouted Miss Luvenia, the oldest woman with us. "We hit the jackpot today. That's a mulberry tree in front of that empty house over there." She reached up and adjusted the rag tied around her head to catch the sweat from her brow. She was sweating like crazy.

"Good looking out!" the ladies shouted as they hurried over to the tree.

"Here we go 'round the mulberry tree early in the morning," the children sang as everybody ran toward the tree.

The women shook the tree while the children gathered berries. It was raining mulberries.

I felt like the guy who yelled, "Land ho!" or Christopher Columbus when he first came to America.

With all containers filled, we happily marched home singing, "When Johnny comes marching home again, hurrah, hurrah! We'll give him a hearty welcoming, hurrah, hurrah!" Picking berries has been fun, and now our morning work is done, hurrah, hurrah!"

Mama hadn't gone berry picking with us but she sure was happy and smiled big when she saw my bucket full of berries.

"Ya'll did good for the first time picking blackberries," she said.

"We got mulberries too!" I said. I told her all about the big mulberry tree down in the woods as she washed and cooked the berries. In no time she had canned them in Ball jars and screwed a gold metal ring around the lid.

She left some berries in the pot and made dumplings to eat with them by dropping balls of dough in the pot.

Canned foods were supposed to be eaten in winter but we ate those berries before the end of that month. "Blackberries and dumplings! Mulberry pies! Yummy, yum, yum!" I shouted to my little sisters when I smelled the aroma of berries. The look on their faces showed me they were afraid to taste mulberries. So I said, "Don't frown before you eat some for yourself."

Life without my daddy was like a bad dream. I wondered when I'd wake up and find that I had been sleeping for a long time.

"Lord, when will we go back home?" I asked. I guess I fell asleep before he answered.

CHAPTER 3

ON SATURDAY MORNING, I leaned over the log fence and watched Grandpa toss a bucket of slop into the trough to feed the two hogs. I frowned as I watched them wagging their little tails on the end of their fat rumps while they went "oink, oink, oink."

"How can crispy fried bacon taste so good when hogs eat all that nasty stuff and wallow in the mud?" I shouted.

"Might look like mess to you, but da hogs like slop," Grandpa answered. He put the slop bucket down, then walked over to the barn to untie Old Bessie as usual. "I gotta feed my cow."

"What's she chewing?" I asked. "Old Bessie looks like she's already found some grass to eat."

"Cows chew the cud."

"The what?" I asked. "I've never heard that word before."

Grandpa leaned over and picked up the pitchfork that he'd knocked over while reaching for the rope to untie Old Bessie. "Dis here pitchfork ought always lean 'gainst the side of da barn. Always turn it backwards like dis." He shoved the pitchfork in the ground covered with hay and pushed the handle against the barn.

"Old Bessie coulda got hurt if she step on it. Huh? What'd ya say? Oh, yeah, yeah, yeah, I 'member now. Let's see how I kin splain myself. The cud is... umm... grass the cow already done swallowed and she spit it back up to chew it some mo."

"Grandpa, did you make that up? That made no sense to me. How can somebody eat throw-up? Yuk!"

"You chillen got a lot to learn about God's creatures," he said as he limped over to untie Old Bessie so she could roam around in her little fenced area next to the barn. That evening, Old Bessie was lying on her side when Grandpa went to tie her up. He leaned over and slapped her belly but she didn't move.

"Oh Lawdy," Grandpa moaned, "Old Bessie done breathed her last."

"What's wrong with her? I asked as I climbed through the fence and carefully tiptoed around piles of manure as I went over to stand beside Grandpa.

"I reckon she died from 'hollow tail' disease. We gotta bury her," Grandpa said.

"Why don't you butcher her like you did that hog and eat the meat?" I asked.

"Ya can't eat no parts of a dead cow ya don't butcher," Grandpa said. "If ya eat the beef from a dead cow, the same thing that killed her might kill you too."

"Ohhhh, it makes sense now that you put it like that Grandpa," I said.

With Old Bessie gone, that was the end of our fresh milk every morning. I soon learned that Old Bessie's milk was a lot thicker than store-bought milk. Grandpa said bought milk is "watered-down."

* * *

A few weeks after Old Bessie had died, I was walking beside Grandpa as he carried the slop bucket back into the house after feeding the hogs. I knew he would set it down beside the kitchen stove and dump in more table scraps and other stuff to attract plenty of flies. As we walked I looked up at him and told him what was on my mind.

"Grandpa, I wish Mama and Daddy got along like you and Grandma. We moved out here 'cause they don't like each other."

"Well now, my lil Justine is da apple of my eye. We been together ever since hatchet was a hammer." He laughed at his own joke.

I laughed too, even though I didn't fully understand what he meant. I just assumed they'd been together for a real long time, almost fifty years, I think. I looked around to make sure that nobody would hear what I was about to say. Then I looked up at Grandpa.

"Did you and grandma ever fight like Mama and Daddy used to?"

"Look at me," Grandpa said with a huge grin on his face. "Don't ya know a big man like me could hurt my lil wife if I hit her? Nope. Me and your grandma git along jes fine. Ain't no need ta fight. She's good ta me."

Just then I heard Mama call me, so I turned around and ran back up the hill. I looked back and shouted, "I'll see you later, Grandpa." I knew I probably had to fix dinner plates for everybody like I usually did after Mama finished cooking. Maybe I need to make more bottles of Carnation baby formula with boiling hot water, I thought. Whatever it was, Mama mostly called me when it was time for me to do some chores. If I finished them, she just made up some more things for me to do. So I took my good ole sweet time finishing my work.

"I'm coming!" I hollered as I ran toward our back door.

* * *

I got used to waking up around six o'clock in the morning to the distant sound of Grandpa starting up his rickety black '56 Ford pickup. The same rattling sound we heard early in the morning was the same sound we heard when he returned around six o'clock in the evening. We could set our clock by my grandpa's going and coming.

Like clockwork Grandma Cox had a hot dinner waiting on the stove for her husband when he came home from work. She called it 'supper' when she fixed grits instead of rice. Grandma set the table for two and sometimes she let me help her. I smiled when she got just as excited as we did at the sound of Grandpa's truck pulling into the driveway in the evening.

Today, as Grandpa pulled into the driveway, she quickly untied her soiled apron and rushed to put on a fresh one. She dabbed a bit of red lipstick on her bottom lip and smeared it with her top lip. She stared at herself in the mirror for a moment, wiped the excess lipstick from around her lips with her fingertip, and then patted her hair to make it lay down flat. By the time Grandpa reached the house, she was standing at the front door holding his slippers in her hand.

"Hey, Jerry!" she smiled.

Grandpa leaned down and kissed her on her cheek. "Something sure smells good in here," he said as he limped across the living room wooden floor to their bedroom.

I knew Grandpa was talking about the aroma coming from the kitchen even though Grandma had dabbed a little bit of perfume behind her ears. Grandma followed close behind him. He plopped down on his twin bed, leaned over, untied and tugged at his cracked, tan brogan boots until each one slid off his foot. Grandma stood nearby waiting to see if he needed help. Sometimes his bad leg hurt too much for him to take off his own boots.

The moment each musty foot was released from its dirty boot, Grandma snuffed out the lingering odor by pushing a brown corduroy slipper over the foot that had just stunk up the room. I laughed as I watched Grandma cover up foot odor as quickly as I could swat a fly that tried to land on my plate.

Next, Grandpa limped straight to their bathroom to freshen up with the warm water Grandma had already run in the bathroom sink.

They were smart to add on a bathroom to their blockhouse, I thought.

The weather had been hot all day. I guess that's why Grandpa dipped both of his big hands in the sink and splashed water over his face and neck. Grandma stood in the bathroom doorway behind him ready to hand him a clean white hand towel.

"Thank ya, Hun," my 6'4" Grandpa said in his gruff voice and then smiled. He leaned down real low and gently pecked his 4'9" wife on the cheek.

Grandma giggled and said, "You welcome, Jerry."

I think that peck on Grandma's cheek made her day 'cause after she received it she turned and went back to the kitchen to fix Grandpa's dinner plate.

Grandma hardly ever said much to anybody. Most of the time, she spent her entire day cooking, cleaning, washing clothes, and ironing. But she spent all evening treating Grandpa like he was a king. Every day she fixed his food, picked up his plate after he ate, propped pillows behind his head, fluffed his pillow, threw a quilt over him while he napped in his favorite chair, and ran his bath water. They seemed to have no worries at all. The only thing that bothered me was that they slept in separate beds in the small bedroom adjacent to the bathroom they had added to their house. I didn't understand why they had twin beds when Mama and Daddy slept in one big double bed.

I liked watching my grandparents show affection. They were complete opposites of Mama and Mr. Fred. The two of them were disgusting together.

"Marriage must be a beautiful thing when the husband and wife love each other," I told myself. "If Mama and Daddy had behaved like my grandparents, then my family would still be together." I fought back tears. Then I thought about all the fights between Mama and Daddy. I'm glad Mama didn't kill Daddy, I thought.

After Grandpa freshened up, he limped over to take his seat in a wooden chair at the round kitchen table covered with a red-and-white checkered tablecloth. I heard a loud grunt as his weight shifted from his feet to the chair. He reached for the tall crystal salt-and-pepper shakers in the center of the table. I knew exactly what he wanted so I helped him out by sliding the salt-and-pepper shakers closer to his right hand. I pushed the shakers toward him

and Grandpa laughed. His "Ha, Ha, Ha" reminded me of
Santa Claus' "Ho, Ho, Ho." Grandpa stared at me with
his mouth open.

"You chillen know what I like jes like my lil wife!"
he said.

"We sure do," I said, smiling. I wondered if Grandma
was going to invite me to join them for dinner today.
Sometimes she did and other times Grandma hinted that
she wanted to be alone with her husband. She'd say, "I
think your Mama needs you at home," rather than just
telling me to go home.

"Sit down. Lemme fix ya a plate," Grandma said after
I put the shakers in Grandpa's reach.

"Yes ma'am!" I said. This was one of those days
when I was going to enjoy a stew beef and potato dinner
with them, and Grandma's homemade biscuits.

As I pulled out the wooden chair to sit down, I
realized that it didn't take me long to figure out when
Grandma wanted me to leave. I smiled as I thought about
the first time Grandma said Mama wanted me. I ran home
wondering how Grandma heard Mama's voice when I
didn't hear a thing.

"Grandma said you called me," I panted.

Mama laughed and said, "My mama always told us,
'Go somewhere and sit down' or 'Go outside and play'
when she wanted to be alone with her husband."

"Ohhhhh, so that's why I didn't hear you calling me.
I get it now," I said.

When the plates were on the table with huge portions
on Grandpa's plate and enough food for a mouse to eat
on Grandma's, it was time to pray over the meal. I liked
to hear Grandpa say the grace. He stared at us without
saying a word and then everybody at the table bowed their
heads and closed their eyes while we held hands.

"Grace in the kitchen, grace in the hall, please for
God's sake, don't eat it all," was Grandpa's favorite
prayer. That was a funny prayer because he always ate
all his food. When Grandpa finished praying he didn't

eat until Grandma said a Bible verse. Her favorite verses were "Jesus wept" and "the Lord is my shepherd."

"Amen," we all said in unison at the end of prayer time.

While Grandpa was eating, I saw moist food rolling around inside his mouth when he talked. He always had plenty to share about his day at work. Then when his plate was empty, he leaned back in his chair, pounded his chest with his fists, gave a loud burp, and said, "Dat was good eatin!" It hit the spot."

His words made Grandma's face light up like a street light in Marshall Village. Grandma blushed and said, "Thank you, Jerry."

My grandpa knew just what to say to make his wife feel good. I wish somebody had taught my daddy to treat his wife like Grandpa treated Grandma. I guess that's what happens when a boy grows up without his father being around to teach him how to be a man.

For some strange reason I asked myself, "Why doesn't Grandpa ever ask Grandma how she spent her day?" Immediately, I answered my own question. I guess he thinks women who stay at home everyday don't have much to talk about.

As soon as they finished eating, Grandpa got up and went outside or somewhere to do some work. I wanted to follow him but today I stayed and helped Grandma clean the dirty dishes and store food in the Frigidaire refrigerator.

What a peaceful life they have, I thought. It's nice having a perfect couple living next door, even though it is too late to help Mama and Daddy.

* * *

One Monday evening while I was reading the book, *Little Women,* I heard Grandpa's truck pull into the driveway. I jumped up from the sofa, carefully laid my book face down on the kitchen table, and ran toward the back door to greet him. Mama stood in the kitchen doorway watching as my little sisters hurried outside so they could be standing at the door of the truck the moment Grandpa opened it. We never knew when he had a treat for us. My little sisters and Harry jumped up and down with excitement as we all rushed to claim a spot.

As I stepped out the kitchen door, I glanced back and cried, "Mama, I love your daddy!"

Mama briefly shook her head as if she were both shocked and insulted. She had a strange look on her face.

I abruptly turned and asked, "Mama, don't you love your daddy too?"

That's when Mama started talking about a family secret that forced me to listen.

"Let me tell you about your Grandpa that you love so much," Mama said. I stared at her as she watched Grandpa get out of the truck surrounded by her children. "My papa cheated on my mama and she left him and moved to Columbia." Mama moved one step toward me. "That's when Mama bought this property out here and moved to Columbia. Papa followed her here. That's why my family ended up moving away from Orangeburg."

Then, almost as if talking to herself she added, "I was glad they moved too. I didn't want to talk country like the people down home. Your grandpa – that you think can do no wrong – had a baby by Mama's best girlfriend."

I gasped as I listened to Mama telling me, of all people, bad things about my grandpa.

"Yeah, I got a sister down home," Mama said. "Papa was still down in Orangeburg when my brother Ezekiel built the house down the hill for mama and this one for himself. Even though Justine Cox swore she'd never trust her Jerry again, she took him back so he could help her raise my five brothers. Papa never spent much time with his sons but he always treated me special." Mama took another step closer to the door while I was standing on the ground. "My brothers ran away to the Army to get away from Mama and farm work. Papa talks tough but Mama mostly raised us by herself." Mama laughed and said, "My mama pinched my brothers' ears 'til they hollered.

Pinching the ears made them boys do whatever she told them to do."

I felt a piercing pain like somebody stabbing me in the heart as Mama kept on talking. She stepped over the threshold, and stood on the ground facing me, still tattling on her papa. I briefly glanced behind me and saw my sisters and Harry walking down the hill with Grandpa. I wondered what he was sharing with them. That's when I realized I'd missed something Mama had said and that she had a lot more to say. A whole lot more.

I forced myself to listen to the ugly things Mama was saying about the papa who loved her. She kept right on talking as if her secret had been locked in her heart for a million years and she was free at last to share it. Words poured out of her like running water.

* * *

"I'll never forget the day when I was a little girl and Mama sent me back home to fetch water," Mama said. "We'd been out in the field cutting sugar cane all morning and it was around noon. I passed the rain barrel that sat at the corner of the house and happened to go inside. I don't remember what for. That's when I saw bare feet in mama and papa's bed. It puzzled me to see feet sticking out the foot of the bed. I stopped and counted one, two, three feet sticking out from 'neath the covers. I knew mama was out in the field."

Mama laughed as she reflected on the incident. Then she said, "I ran back out the door. I filled that jug up as fast as I could and hurried back to the field before mama came looking for me." She laughed again as I stared at her. It was hard to believe my mama was talking to me about real serious stuff.

"What's wrong with married people?" I shouted. "Do people marry just so they can have somebody to cheat on? Why don't they just stay single?"

"People like excitement in their lives," Mama said. "Some people just like to live dangerously. I want you to know your Grandpa ain't perfect. You look at him like he's a god, or something. He's a man just like your daddy. The only difference is that my papa is old and worn out now."

At that moment, I think I figured out why Mama and Daddy used to fight—Daddy accused Mama of cheating on him and she accused him of cheating on her. Daddy had already told me long ago how his father had left his mother for another woman. Mama seemed certain that my godmother, Mrs. Nash, cheated on Rev. Nash by going with our pastor, Rev. Hughes, who was married too. "Ummmm."

If Grandpa Cox cheated on his wife too, then why do storybooks always say, "They married and lived happily ever after," before we read, "The End?"

"That's just a lie that sounds good," Mama chuckled.

"Where are the married people who don't cheat?" I asked.

"I don't know any," Mama said. Then she walked back inside while I stood there pondering everything I had just learned. I didn't know what I was supposed to do with this new information about my grandpa. It certainly didn't stop me from loving him.

Right then and there at nine years old, I vowed, "I will marry only one time when I grow up. All of my children will have the same daddy and all of them will look alike. My husband and I will never fight, cheat or separate. We will be faithful to each other until death do us part in our old age." I laughed at myself when I realized I had jokingly quoted Rev. Hughes.

Surely, any man in his right mind ought to appreciate a good wife, I thought. Good people attract good people, don't they? If I'm nice to all the people I meet in the country, on the school bus, and in my new school, then I should have lots of good friends. That's just the way things ought to be.

I guess the bad news about my grandpa made me think about my daddy. I tried to imagine the day when my family would come together again like my grandparents came back together. If Grandpa cheated on his wife and now they're happily married, then it's possible that my family can get back together too. Oh, how happy I would be.

That Friday night I cried as I lay in bed thinking about my Daddy and the way life used to be before we came to live in the country. Mr. Fred was in Mama's bedroom and I couldn't fall asleep, so I got up and sat in the matching pleather chair and propped my feet up in one of our wooden kitchen chairs. I struggled to get comfortable enough to sleep sitting upright in the chair with a pillow tucked behind my head. I simply couldn't force myself to fall asleep.

As I sat staring at the darkness and listening to the loud snores from Mr. Fred and Mama, I began sulking and talking to myself. "That ole drunk Mr. Fred sleeping in Mama's bed is the reason my daddy's gone. If Mama only knew how uncomfortable it is not to have a decent place to lay my head! How can they sleep peacefully while I'm still wide awake?" The more I sulked, the more I thought about the way my family used to live before we ended up in the country.

I wondered if Daddy felt bad about leaving us. I guess he forgot that he told us, "I don't want to be like my daddy who left me and my mama to get along the best way we could. I want to be the kind of daddy who stays with my family until I die."

"Daddy lied to us!" I cried angrily. "He's not here and he's not dead." Then I remembered Daddy had clearly said, "I hated the hard life we lived after my daddy left us."

"Now I know what he was talking about. I hate living like this too!" I mumbled.

A warm tear trickled down my cheek. I wiped it with my index finger and buried my face in the pillow. I silently screamed and yawned. It seemed useless to hope Mama and Daddy will get back together when Mr. Fred is always coming around.

Then my mind drifted all the way back to the stories my daddy told us a hundred times before. ...

CHAPTER 4

I LAY ON MY BACK on my sofa bed in the living room staring at the darkness. I kept thinking about all the things Daddy had told us about his hard life while growing up in the country down in Bamberg and Orangeburg. I missed that warm, fuzzy feeling I had when I sat at his feet, especially on Sunday afternoons when he told us stories.

"I can't believe we're living the same way Daddy did a long time ago," I whispered. "How I wish he'd come and take me out of this place." I put my hand on my cheek and shook my head.

I pictured Sunday afternoons with my daddy. That was always story time in our house. My brother and younger sisters and I squeezed in around Daddy's feet on the living room floor as Daddy rocked in his squeaky wooden rocking chair. Although I hung onto Daddy's every word, my mouth-watered as the smells of good food from Mama's steaming pots on the kitchen stove and sugar biscuits in the oven floated from the kitchen and filled the air in the living room.

Daddy started his story in a low voice. "I was five years old on that cold and rainy Saturday afternoon in November 1925 when I witnessed the last big fight between my mama, Susie, and my papa, Bubba Kincaid. I was having fun riding my stick pony from the front door to the back door of our shotgun house that sat a ways off the road. I hopped through the living room, past the bedroom and past the kitchen then turned 'round 'cause if I'd kept on hopping in a straight line I woulda ended up at the outdoor toilet down the path."

"When I turned 'round to hop back down the hall I heard my mama and papa in the kitchen. My mama started shouting at him and I said to myself, "It's fight time again."

I hopped faster and faster as they shouted louder and louder back and forth. When I reached the bedroom, I brought my pony to a screeching halt and jumped off, leaving it leaning against the wall in the hall. I dashed in the bedroom and crawled into my usual spot under the bed where I always ran when things got rough in my house.

"Everybody knows 'bout you and Charlotte!" My mama yelled. "You got a wife and a son. Don't you got no shame?"

"You can't tell me how to run my life!" Papa fired back. "I'm grown! I do what I want to do with whoever I please!"

"I slid further back against the wall underneath the metal frame of my twin bed. It sat cater-corner to my parents' double bed. I crouched there with my fingers stuck in my ears to block out the loud shouts that rattled the windows, but I could still hear them fussing."

Daddy showed us how he stuck his index fingers in his ears.

"I'm tired of you cheating on me! I'm sick a you!" Mama yelled at Papa.

"Lots of women want me!" Papa shouted back. "I don't have to stay with you!"

"Suddenly, it grew real quiet. I waited to hear something. Then Papa stomped into the bedroom. I quietly stretched out on the floor and lifted the fringe of my bedspread just enough to get a peek at the whole room. I fixed my gaze on Papa's Brogan boots and followed them. Papa leaned over and pulled a worn-out tan leather suitcase from under his bed and tossed it on top. The floor squawked as Papa stomped to the chifforobe. He grabbed some clothes from the bottom draw, threw them in the suitcase, and slammed it shut. He clutched that tattered suitcase handle in one hand, and with the other he snatched his favorite wide-brimmed black Stetson hat wrapped in plastic off the nail next to the door."

"I watched him storm out of the bedroom like a streak of lightning cross the sky. I heard Papa cussing at the front door 'cause it wouldn't open right away. He knew good and well that wood door got sticky and was hard to open when it rained. He yanked the front door real hard and it squeaked open. Then he slammed it shut behind him but it bounced back open. I ran out of the bedroom just in time to see one of the three windowpanes in the door rattle, fall on the living room floor and break in a million pieces."

Papa yelled, "I'm GONE!"

"I ran through the pile of glass, pushed the front door all the way open and watched my papa slosh up the muddy path leading to the road. If he'd looked back just one time he woulda seen me standing in the doorway. I watched him walk away step-by-step as rainwater filled his boot prints along the path between the hedges. My parents had argued many times before and sometimes papa had walked out, but this was the first time he left with a suitcase."

"He didn't even tell me goodbye," Daddy mumbled, then dropped his head.

That's the part of his story that made me cry. I looked around and saw Harry and my sisters wiping their eyes too.

"Papa disappeared when he reached the main road like a dream when you wake up in the morning," Daddy said.

He paused and took a deep breath before he continued his story. "After my papa walked out of sight, I tiptoed down the hall so the loose floor boards wouldn't squawk too loud as I headed for the kitchen."

"I stood in the kitchen door watching my mama stare at the wall. She had her two elbows on the round wood table and her head propped up on her two cupped-hands like this." Daddy put one hand on each cheek to show us how his mama had her head propped up. We did the same thing.

Daddy gave a deep sigh before he continued. "I saw tears crawl down my mama's cheek. I think she saw me standing in the door out of the corner of her eye 'cause right then she lifted a corner of her apron and wiped away her tears. She kept on looking straight ahead, but she stood up quickly, walked over to a shelf on the wall and took down a big brown ceramic mixing bowl. She leaned down and scooped up a homemade tin cup full of flour from a ten-pound sack in the tin grocery can on the floor and poured it in the mixing bowl on the table."

"I knew Mama was gonna make some biscuits, and I knew she wasn't gonna talk about her fight with Papa. I was standing there with tears in my eyes looking up at my mama. I wanted her to hug me, say something to me, anything, but she didn't say one word. She just acted like she didn't see me at all. I was hurting so bad inside but I couldn't bring myself to say nothing either. I reckon I had something to be glad about because I still had my mama. So I turned and went back down the hall and sat on the edge of my bed and cried my eyes out while mama stayed in the kitchen cooking."

"I could hear my mama in the kitchen just a-singing and a-crying, *'I will trust in the Lord, I will trust in the Lord, I will trust in the Lord, 'til I die. I will trust in the Lord, I will trust in the Lord, I will trust in the Lord, 'til I die'.*"

Daddy suddenly stopped singing and looked around at us and said, "I would NEVER leave my family like my daddy left us. Ya'll are stuck with me like white on rice from now on."

"YEAII! That's my Daddy!" Harry cheered, waving his fists in the air.

"Daddy, tell us what happened next?" I asked anxiously.

"Well," Daddy continued, "two weeks after papa walked out, mama invited her older sister, Nadine, to come live with us. She was a widow with no children. That means she had a dead husband. The only thing she brought with her was a green metal trunk full of memories of her late husband and some clothes. Aunt Nadine was good company for her little sister. She helped out with farming the land and was like a second mama to me."

"I always wondered where Papa had gone but I didn't ask 'cause children knew better than to question grown folks back in those days. But one day I overheard my mama say she was my papa's second wife. She told Aunt Nadine, 'Bubba Kincaid musta got tangled up in Charlotte's long black wavy hair'."

"I thought 'tangled up in hair' meant just that. In my mind, I saw my papa wrapped up in some long thick ropes trying hard to get loose so he could come back home. That sure would explain why nobody ever saw or heard from him after he walked out that Saturday."

"My Aunt Nadine didn't let me get away with nothing! Every time I thought 'bout doing something wrong I heard, "David! David!" Daddy mimicked Nadine's raspy voice.

We laughed as he showed us how she called his name in a croaking voice that sounded like a frog. "David." Then he went on with his story after we stopped laughing.

"Aunt Nadine sure knew how to keep busy. Every day she saw to it that I had chores and they never changed from week-to-week. Monday was washday. When it rained, I slung wet clothes over the doors and the backs of chairs instead of on the clothesline. Tuesday was ironing day. Sometimes heating the iron in the fireplace had terrible results. I scorched a big hole in more than one pair of my underpants. So I know what it is to 'be ye holy' like the preacher say."

"One of my jobs was to fill the water bottle so clothes could be sprinkled before ironing. Sometimes I rolled up my overalls in Argo starch and put 'em in the icebox. Since Aunt Nadine loved to iron so much, I let her iron the ceases in all my pants. Wednesday was mending day. My mama said she and Aunt Nadine had old eyes so they needed my fresh pair of eyes to thread their needles. Thursday was churning day. I liked playing with the pole in the wooden barrel churn we used to make butter. Ya'll need to know we get butter from cow milk. Churning seemed more like fun than work. My mama and auntie carefully molded the butter into thick chunks like bricks and wrapped them in wax paper. Sometimes people came over our house to buy a chunk of butter for a dime. Friday was cleaning day, both inside and outside. I had to sweep the yard. Saturday was bake day as well as the day to get everything ready for church the next day. My job was to polish shoes so everybody's feet would look good in our Sunday clothes. We had to dress up to go to church to meet King Jesus. A-L-L day Sunday was church day."

"The other children at church liked to stick around me so they could be amongst the first to taste the cakes and pies from our kitchen. One of the old church mothers called mama's butter-rich Pound Cake and Aunt Nadine's scrumptious Red Velvet Cake *shamefully good.*"

"I had a rough time growing up doing all them chores I had to do every day the good Lord sent come rain or shine. But I learned how to work hard for a living. After papa left us, I learned how to scatter chicken feed, slop the hogs, lead the cow out of the barn and bring it back from the pasture, fetch firewood, shoo the hens away so I could gather chicken eggs, kill and clean chickens, and sweep the yard with a stick broom. I had to learn how to say my weekly Bible verse from memory too or get popped in the mouth by mama's hand. If I missed one word she'd start yelling at me."

"David, pay attention when somebody's teaching you something! How else you gonna learn?"

Daddy smiled when he said, "The two women in my house told me they believed all work and no play would make me a dull boy. But how could I play when they kept me busy working all day long? The only fun things I did was play kickball, ride a pony, shoot marbles, and climb trees."

"Is that why you laughed so hard the first time you played hopscotch with me?" I asked.

"Yeah, girl," Daddy said. "That game was new to me. That's the first time I ever played a girl's game. I was having fun doing all that jumping around. When I was a boy, I had just a few friends at church and in my grammar school next door to the church cemetery."

"Matter-of-fact, in the fifth grade, I used to play with a boy in my class name Skinny Wesley. His papa was a sharecropper. One day Skinny Wesley asked me to come work in the cotton fields so I could make some spending money. The first time I had some coins jangling in my pocket made me feel like I was a grown man. After that first payday is when I started playing hooky from school and went to work in the fields. For a long time, I pretended to go to school but I didn't. I figured, what my mama and auntie didn't know wouldn't hurt 'em."

"Since nobody in my house mentioned Bubba Kincaid's name, the memory of my papa faded as the years passed. After awhile I forgot all about him as the women in my life took his place."

"I liked the way Aunt Nadine always found something good to say 'bout me and make me feel like a strong man. She praised me for doing my chores without being reminded, for saying 'thank you' and 'you welcome' and always saying, 'Yes ma'am' or 'No ma'am,' and for holding the doors open for my elders."

"My mama liked to say, 'Son, you look real handsome in your church clothes.' Yep, my mama knew just what to say to make a man feel good. Too bad my papa didn't 'preciate her."

"She must have told me every Sunday, 'Son, you gonna make some lucky girl a fine husband one day'."

"I felt proud about providing a strong helping hand to the two women I loved and who loved me. Even as a young man I made up my mind that my wife would stay home and take care of our babies while I went to work to provide for my family. Life in our home was peaceful and good for years until that summer day when my whole world caved in."

* * *

I rubbed my eyes as daylight seeped through the closed venetian blinds.

Thinking about that story made me mad at Daddy because he acted a whole lot like his papa. I wondered if Daddy even remembered he promised us he would never leave his family.

Why, why, why do we have to live just like Daddy did when he was a boy? I hate it! I hate it! I groaned under my breath.

I gazed at the light as the sun peeped through the venetian blinds. A light beam shaped like a funnel came shining through the blinds. I stared at the light beam because I saw dust stirring around inside the light when nobody was sweeping. Then the thought that came to my mind surprised me. Like dust in the air that can only be seen in the sunlight, nobody really knows how much they're like their parents on the inside until they grow up. We can't see the resemblance when we're young.

"Oh, no!" I cried. "I know I don't want to have a whole lot of babies like my mama. I know that for sure!"

CHAPTER 5

ON A HOT SATURDAY AFTERNOON, I sat in the
metal swing on the front porch reading a Wonder Woman
comic book while my little sisters played in the yard. I
wished Wonder Woman would come and rescue me from
the country and take me back to the people and home that
I loved.

Something didn't seem right! After Daddy left we had
not one, not two, but three new babies added to our family
in the same year. I couldn't believe my sisters wanted to
copy Mama by having babies too!"

In a way I envied my oldest sister, Zenobia, because
she managed to completely escape life in the country. She
said she wasn't moving to the country and she didn't. I
still remember that night around the kitchen table when
she looked up and told Mama, "I wrote Abraham a letter
and told him I'm pregnant. "He said, *You're going to be
my wife because I love you. I will take care of you and the
baby.* I'll show you what he wrote in his letter if you want
to see it."

"Here!" She shoved the letter into Mama's hand. "So
I'm going to stay right here in Marshall Village with my
friend Earline until Abraham comes home. I don't do
outhouses even when I'm NOT pregnant!"

"Well, I hope he told you the truth," Mama said. "If
you change your mind you know where to find us."

I was over at Grandpa's house the same evening we
moved to the country when my big sister Lynette came
flying through the front door weeping and wailing like
somebody had just died. I watched her from the kitchen
doorway as she fussed at the dial on the telephone for
turning too slow. She finally finished dialing the number.

"Hurry up!" she shouted while the phone was ringing. Tears were streaming down her cheeks the whole time she waited for somebody to answer the phone. I'd never seen her that upset before. Her hand was shaking as she shouted in the receiver, "Roscoe, I can't do this! My belly is too big for me to sit on a little night pot! It's all your fault! You've got to come and get me out of here!" There was a long pause and then she slammed the receiver back on the hook and walked slowly out the door. I don't think she ever noticed me watching her.

I reckon Roscoe got the picture because he showed up early Sunday morning, banging on the front door and yelling, Mrs. Kincaid! Mrs. Kincaid!"

"I'm coming!" Mama hollered. "You can stop making all that racket."

I jumped up when Mama opened the front door.

"Mrs. Kincaid," Roscoe said, "I've come to take your daughter to be my wife. After we get married we're going to move to Brooklyn, New York. I promise to take good care of her and our baby."

Mama picked up the suitcase Lynette had put beside the door Saturday night. She stepped out on the porch with it in her hand and set it down on the porch.

"She's coming now," Mama said. "Everybody ain't cut out for this kind of life, you know. You're a good church boy, so I know you'll take good care of my daughter."

"Yes Ma'am. I'm going to do just that," Roscoe promised.

As soon as Lynette wobbled through the front door with her ponytail swishing from side to side, I ran behind her in my pajamas to pat her round belly before she walked down our one step. She looked pretty in her lavender maternity top and white shorts. She had a cute fake lavender flower that looked like a real one stuck in her long ponytail. I didn't know whether I should laugh or cry to see her leave, so I just walked alongside her while Roscoe walked ahead of us carrying her suitcase.

He opened the trunk and tossed her suitcase inside then rushed over to open the passenger door for her. I stood nearby watching while Roscoe helped her get in his gray Ford Fairlane.

"Are you all right, Lynn?" he asked before he closed the door.

"I am now," she said as she scooted back in her seat." She looked up at him and smiled.

She's so pretty, I thought. I liked the way Roscoe treated her like his princess. That's the way I want to be treated when I grow up, I thought.

I leaned over and whispered, "I'm going to miss you." My bottom lip quivered as soon as the words escaped my mouth. I felt tears well up in my eyes. It hurt to see my family falling apart even more.

"You're welcome to come visit us in New York," Lynette said.

"Really?" I asked. I couldn't believe a little girl could travel such a long way from home.

"Write me and I'll answer," she said as she settled down in the front seat. "I'll write first to send you my address."

"Okay," I said.

Mama and I waved goodbye as Roscoe backed the car out of the driveway and sped away.

"God, please let them get to New York in one piece," I prayed. "Because I want to go visit them."

* * *

Abraham came home from the Air Force around the end of June. Five days later he brought Zenobia to the house to tell Mama they got married and they moved into a duplex in Ridgewood. I think I saw what love looked like when I saw the smile on Abraham's face as he helped Zenobia climb the one step to our front porch. Zenobia waddled across the porch like a duck with Abraham holding her hand. I was proud to hold the screen door open for them.

"This is my husband, Abraham," Zenobia proudly announced. I smiled at the way he quickly stepped behind her as soon as he realized the door wasn't wide enough for them to enter side-by-side. I heard claps behind me coming from Harry and my little sisters and glanced back to see them lined up on the porch.

Why didn't I think of that? I thought. A new husband was a great big announcement. I clapped late but I still felt proud to celebrate the good news. I felt excited to see my first newlywed couple and handsome Abraham in his starched khaki Air Force uniform. Seeing the way they stuck together reminded me of the comic strip characters Mutt and Jeff and I smiled to myself.

"And this is my pumpkin, I mean, my wife," Abraham teased.

Zenobia lifted her hand and gently touched his lips with her index finger. He smiled at her. I followed them inside after they passed me. Zenobia's face lit up like a light bulb as she waddled like a duck alongside Abraham, holding onto his arm until she sat down on the sofa. Her stomach looked like a round watermelon about to pop open. The smiles on their faces sent a warm shiver down my spine.

"I hope you two stay happy like this all the time!" I said. "Love is a pretty picture. I like it!" I held my head high and strutted out the front door as soon as Mama entered the living room. I wanted to keep my good feeling just in case Zenobia and Mama argued. Zenobia and Abraham talked with Mama for a long time after I left the room and nobody raised their voice.

As the newlyweds were leaving, April ran across the driveway behind Abraham's blue Buick while he was backing up.

"Get your butt out of the way!" I hollered.

Abraham abruptly stopped the car.

"Come here, Davida!" Zenobia yelled. I ran to the passenger side of the car thinking she was going to thank me for keeping Abraham from hitting April.

"Don't you ever say a bad word again!" she yelled.

I was shocked. After that I was scared of getting a whupping for saying the word butt, and I didn't even know it was a cuss word. I remembered that Zenobia whupped us as hard as Daddy. So I stammered, "I won't. I'm sorry."

"You ought to be sorry!" Zenobia shot a mean look at me and said, "I'll see you later." She turned to Abraham and said nicely, "Now we can leave, Honey."

I stepped back from the car and Abraham finished backing out of the driveway. I stood watching them drive away. I felt like I had done something terrible. I was confused. All I tried to do was save my little sister's life, I thought. I didn't understand why she fussed at me and not April.

When Zenobia's baby boy, Sylvester, was born on July 25, my sister Beverly went to live with them to help out. Beverly told me all the arrangements had been made the day Zenobia and Abraham had that long talk with Mama. Beverly knew too but kept it a secret from me.

To my unpleasant surprise, I had been promoted to the eldest child at home.

The very next month, Mama got a letter from Lynette saying her son, Brandon, was born in Brooklyn on August 18. I squealed with joy.

"I wanted all boys," Mama said, "but I got mostly girls and my girls have the boys. Boys go in the service and send money home to their mama like my brothers did."

My feelings were hurt when she said that. I guess Mama would appreciate all of my hard work around the house if I were a boy, I thought. "God, why didn't you make me a boy?" I asked. God didn't answer me so I just went on outside and started playing with my little sisters. Harry had gone up the road to play with his friends like he usually did. I resented Harry's freedom because boys were always free to go off and play while girls had to stay at home where there was always work to do.

"Why can Harry go to his friend's house and get away with not doing his fair share of the work around here?" I complained to Mama.

Mama snapped back, "Harry can go off when he wants to 'cause boys don't bring babies home."

"They just leave their babies with the girl," I said under my breath while walking out of the room.

"One day I'm leaving here and going to New York!" I proudly announced to the skinny girl staring at me from the mirror behind our bedroom door. "You just watch and see!"

I didn't like taking Zenobia's place as the oldest child at home. No wonder she was sassy. I don't think it's right for a child to have to take care of little children unless they have a babysitting job that pays some money. I'm a child too and I want to have some fun.

CHAPTER 6

A FEW DAYS AFTER HEARING about the birth of Lynette's son, I was bubbling with excitement once again. I gobbled down my grits and crispy fatback bacon on a hot August morning, my first day of fourth grade in my new school. I brushed my teeth in a hurry and then rushed outside for my first school bus ride. Although I knew I looked cute in my new yellow sundress that Mama had made, I felt knots in my stomach when I thought of meeting my new classmates and teacher for the first time.

"Davida, here comes the bus!" the other children yelled.

I felt beads of perspiration on my forehead as I ran up the hill where my friends were standing on red clay beside the pavement. A cluster of metal mailboxes, each with a red flag, was the designated school bus stop.

Brakes squealed as the big yellow school bus came to a stop. I was the last one to climb the bus steps before the high school student driver pulled a lever to close the double doors behind me. The bus suddenly jerked and I lunged forward, tossing from side-to-side as I headed down the narrow aisle looking for a vacant window seat. After I sat down, I pressed my face against the glass and watched the trees fly past the window.

Yea! I'm glad I've got somewhere else to go, I thought.

That first morning I realized that catching the school bus to Wardlow Elementary every morning was going to be a lot more challenging than walking to Marshall Village Elementary. I had plenty of time to think about a lot of things while sitting quietly in my seat on the long ride to school.

I was surprised when I walked into my classroom and saw my elderly fourth grade teacher, Mrs. Ruby Hudson Moss. She limped across the wooden planks on the waxed schoolroom floor without a cane. As I watched her limping, I thought about Grandpa Cox who limps with a cane. I wondered what was wrong with her leg.

Not only am I living in the country like Daddy did back in 1925, but my teacher looks like she came from back in the day too, I thought. I gently slapped my cheek to make sure I was awake and not dreaming.

Mrs. Moss was wearing a pretty light gray suit and white blouse with a bow tied around her neck. She looked like she should have worn that suit to church instead of school. Her hair, a mixture of black and gray, was pulled back into a bun that looked a cake doughnut. I didn't know teachers could be so old and have physical disabilities.

During our science lesson, I noticed that Mrs. Moss had lace hanging below the hem of her skirt. I guess she noticed it too because she abruptly stopped talking about animals that roamed the earth long ago.

"I'll be right back," she said softly. Then she rushed behind a wooden partition that ran across the back of the classroom with an opening on each end. On the other side of the partition was a long, narrow cloakroom.

The class was quiet as we all sat waiting for her to come back.

After Mrs. Moss had been gone for a long time, I slid out of my back row seat and tiptoed to the cloakroom entrance opposite the one she had entered. I took a quick peek inside and saw hooks for us to hang our coats and sweaters lined up along both sides of the wall. Below the hooks were cubbyholes and a bottom tray for galoshes and umbrellas. Near the other entrance Mrs. Moss stood bent over, with her back to me, pulling up a pair of long, white-laced bloomers that hung down to her knees. I gasped. Then I rushed back to my seat.

As I slid in my seat, I whispered to the girl seated next to me, "You won't believe what I just saw!"

"Tell me! Tell me!" she pleaded.

"Mrs. Moss is back there pulling up her bloomers!" I said.

That girl quickly whispered to the student next to her and that person whispered to the next, and before I knew it we had played the game of telephone. By the time the last person got the message, the whole class knew I had ratted on the teacher. The buzz in the classroom made me feel very uncomfortable.

A short time later, Mrs. Moss limped back into the classroom apologizing for having to deal with "a problem of popped elastic."

Everyone snickered as she limped toward her desk. There was no more lace below her hem.

"What's so funny?" she asked.

All thirty classmates turned their heads toward me.

Laughing Luther pointed at me and blurted out, "Ask Davida."

"I'm invisible," I told myself while staring stoically at the teacher. I tried my best to ignore my classmates' stares. I had hoped nobody would tell on me. I groaned and slid lower in my seat. If only I could just disappear! I prayed, "God, please don't let me get in trouble on the first day at my new school?"

Mrs. Moss glanced at me over the rim of her thick eyeglasses that hung from her neck on a silver chain. She paused for a moment, then continued where she left off in the science lesson on the vanishing dinosaurs.

I sat on pins and needles until I heard the lunch bell buzz. I breathed a sigh of relief. As soon as I stepped into the hallway, I saw laughing Luther, the class clown, waiting for me.

He was laughing when he pointed at me shouting, "You better be glad nobody told Mrs. Moss you said, "She was back there with her draws down."

"I didn't say that!" I fired back.

"Yes, you did," he said. "Hey, everybody, didn't Davida say she caught Mrs. Moss with her draws down?"

"That's what I heard," my classmates said one after the other as we headed for the lunch line.

"From now on I'll keep my mouth shut. I'll be careful not to say anything that you can say I said when I know I didn't say it," I pouted. "You know how to get people in trouble."

I came to the conclusion that rumors are half-truths or deliberate lies spread by people who either confuse the facts or don't want to know the truth.

When I came to class the following day, Mrs. Moss had assigned me to sit in the front row. "Bright students always sit in front of the class," she said. She smiled and looked straight at me.

I smiled, thinking, she just put me up close so she could keep her eyes on me. Oh well, I guess I deserve it.

During the next few days, Mrs. Moss proved to be a fun and caring teacher. I cherished every kind word she shared and I learned a lot from her. On Friday morning, she handed me my weekly arithmetic test with a big red 100% written across the top of the page. My mouth flew wide open. She put on her eyeglasses and looked straight at me like she always did when she had something important to say.

I looked down at my desk to avoid her gaze.

"Davida, look at me," she said.

I was embarrassed about what she might say, but I looked up through Mrs. Moss' lenses into her dark brown eyes.

"You're going to be successful," she said. "Don't ever let anyone tell you otherwise."

This time I blushed when I realized all eyes were on me. I felt special. Mrs. Moss made me feel so good that I had to fight the urge to jump up and shout like happy people do in church.

While Mrs. Moss limped around passing out more test papers, I was busy imagining myself a teacher, dressed up in pretty clothes and walking around the classroom checking on my students. I'll be a teacher when I grow up – a young one of course, I silently declared. I won't stay at home changing diapers all day and fixing bottles of formula like my mama. My husband and I will have two cars and live in a big pretty house like my friend Caroline who lives across the street from Marshall Village. We'll shop for groceries at a big supermarket together, go to a big church where somebody plays the organ and church bells ring, and pray together before every meal like my grandparents do. We'll talk together and laugh at each other's jokes like my godparents do. We'll only have two children, or maybe three, and they'll all look alike because they'll have the same mama and same daddy. My husband and I will never fight like Mama and Daddy, and we'll live happily ever after like Cinderella and her prince.

When Mrs. Moss finished passing out the test papers, she wrote the top three test scores on the board. My grade of 100% was number one. The second highest score was 75% and the third was 72%.

Wow! I beat everybody in arithmetic! I shouted silently. No wonder Mrs. Moss said kind words to me. When I teach arithmetic I'm going to walk around the classroom helping students work problems. I'll show them step-by-step how to do their work. Yes! I almost blurted out loud, I'm going to be a teacher!

When Mrs. Moss spoke to me, her words sounded like they came straight from God himself. Her confidence in me, of all people, the eighth child of David and Blossom Kincaid, inspired me to aim for making all As that year. There was no doubt in my mind that I could do it.

In Social Studies class, Mrs. Moss said, "My husband was killed in World War II. Losing him hurt so badly that I never wanted to marry anybody else. In his memory I have this flag of the United States of America." She held up a heavy wooden box for us to look through the glass to see the stars and stripes in a sea of red white and blue. Her flag resembled the one we saw hoisted on the flagpole every morning and lowered at the end of each school day.

"Oh, my gosh! Her husband must have been real important to have his own flag!" I silently exclaimed. "No wonder she can wear pretty clothes."

Now, there's a woman who loved her husband. If her husband had not been killed in the war they would still be together. The government sent him away to be killed. Daddy didn't go to war and he and Mama are not together. He just left.

I felt sorry that Mrs. Moss had no children. All she had was her students. All of a sudden, I felt ashamed of myself for having made fun of such a nice lady. I wasn't the typical "class clown" so I wondered why I'd ratted on my teacher. "Did I do it to win new friends?" I asked myself. If I did it for that reason, then I was wrong.

I silently prayed, "God, please forgive me for making fun of my teacher 'cause I wouldn't want anybody to make fun of me."

The next morning while I was helping Mrs. Moss cut out flowers to decorate the bulletin board, I told her that my daddy lived on Divine Street and she got excited.

"Your daddy lives directly across the street from my house," she said. "I'd love to have you come and visit me when you go visit your daddy."

My loyalty to her was sealed from that day forward. I loved my new teacher. Her invitation to visit her at home made me feel extra special. I volunteered to help her with everything she needed to do. By helping her, I could learn how to be a teacher. I helped her sharpen pencils, pass out papers and weekly readers, collect books, and I ran errands. My classmates teased me about being the teacher's pet but I didn't care. I considered myself to be a teacher-in- training. How else could I learn how to be a teacher?

I told Mrs. Moss all about the things that happened to me before we moved to the country and she listened with interest. I don't know who enjoyed our time together the most – the storyteller or the listener.

"You've had an interesting life," Mrs. Moss said. "Your parents' separation caused you to mature quicker than most children your age."

I smiled, but I really didn't understand what she meant.

CHAPTER 7

I PUSHED BACK THE COVERS one morning and saw bumps on my arm. I rubbed my arm with my hand and noticed the same tiny bumps all over my other arm. I sat up on my sofa bed and lifted my pajama top and saw my chest covered with hundreds of bumps. I hopped out of bed and ran into the kitchen in my bare feet and blue flannel pajamas.

"Mama, I've got bumps all over me!" I shouted as soon as I saw her walking toward the kitchen stove with a box of matches and a long piece of wood in her hand.

Mama took one look at me and said, "Those are chill bumps. Nothing serious. These blockhouses hold cold in winter and heat in summer. Let me show you how to make a fire to knock the chill off." She removed one match from the box, closed it again, then struck a match on the side of the box and lit the wood. Black smoke came from the crackling wood that caught fire right away.

"This is called kindling," Mama said. "You use it to start a fire 'cause it burns real fast." She slid the burning kindling beneath the twigs she had already laid crisscross inside the stove pocket. "Watch the fire a little while to make sure it don't go out before you close the stove door."

In a little while, I could feel heat coming from what used to be the cold iron stovetop.

"From now on, make a fire as soon as you get up," she said.

"Yes ma'am," I said. "I can do that since I'm always the first one up anyway."

I stood by the hot stove for a few minutes and the chill bumps went away.

I thought it was strange that our house was cold in winter and hot in summer. I tried to find out why by watching builders add on a room to my friend Elaine's house up the road. They glued concrete blocks together like sandwich cookies with crème in the middle. I stood at a distance watching with interest with my fingers stuck in my ears to drown out the screeching noise from the metal spatula they used to spread cement on top of the blocks and scrape away the excess grit. They made a mud-slinging mess with that mixture of sand and cement they dipped out of a wheelbarrow. I sneaked over and picked up a block off the ground while they weren't looking. It wasn't heavy at all. I noticed that the builders could break a block in no time when they only needed a half of one. Then it occurred to me that blocks aren't as solid as they look.

Hmm... things are not always as they appear. Right then I realized I had been wrong in thinking that the absence of fighting in our house meant that everything was going along just fine. Now I could easily see that it was during the peaceful time that my family fell apart. Mama was seeing Mr. Fred and Daddy was going with Miss Annie Mae. My parents didn't fight any more because both of them were happy doing whatever they wanted to do. It's strange that I learned this lesson by watching builders split a concrete block into two halves.

I sure hope Zenobia and Lynette are happy with their new husbands, I thought, as I walked back home I was also thinking, Mama's brother Ezekiel learned how to build blockhouses for people to live in by practicing with mud cakes. Since somebody had to build houses, Uncle Ezekiel did just that.

When our blockhouse got cold, I found myself building fires in the stove and fireplace even though children were forbidden to play with matches. People make exceptions to the rules when something must be done to meet a need. After my concrete block cutting lesson, I went home with a full understanding of why I was allowed to use matches, make fires, and use an ax to chop down trees. Mama needed my help.

"All right, Harry, let's go do this thing!" I yelled when it was time to gather firewood that afternoon.

"I want my Daddy!" Harry shouted back as usual. "This is a man's job." After he pitched a fit, he reluctantly tagged along behind me pulling a little red wagon.

"I love doing this just as much as you do, but somebody's got to do it," I said as I led the way into the woods with the ax handle propped on my shoulder.

We trekked deep into the wooded acres sprawled behind our grandparents' house and ours. Armed with a long-handled ax and a red-handled hatchet in my hand, we followed a zigzagged path covered with twigs, leaves, and bark until I found the perfect pine to chop down for firewood. It was not too big and not too small.

"Chop, chop, chop," went the sound of the ax against the medium-sized tree as I hewed away at the base. The echo, "chop, chop, chop" whistled through the treetops as a reminder that powerful sounds roam around in the deep woods. I was convinced that the loud sounds warned critters to keep away from us.

I handed the ax to Harry who took a few whacks at the chipped spot when I got tired. After a short break, I resumed chopping until I heard Harry yell, "Timber!"

We looked up to see which way the tree was falling and then ran out of the way. I cut off the branches and chopped up the tree. We loaded the red wagon with logs and headed back home. My brother's main job was to push the wagon up the hill while I pulled.

"My hands feel like they're on fire!" I cried out beneath the strain of pulling the heavy load. Even with Harry pushing the wagon I huffed and puffed like the big bad wolf trying to get to the Three Little Pigs. I kept huffing and puffing as I pulled the wagon all the way up the hill. I could easily tell when Harry stopped pushing because I couldn't make the wagon budge without his help."

"So you do need me for something," Harry said sarcastically. He knew I was glad to have a brother that day.

"You are good for something," I said trying in vain to think of other things he was good at around our house.

Our push and pull worked fine until suddenly the wagon was as light as a feather. It felt like there was no weight at all on the other end of the handle so I glanced back to make sure Harry was still pushing. *This is too good to be true,* I thought at the same moment Harry shrieked, "Stop, Davida!"

I turned around and saw Harry struggling to keep the loaded wagon from rolling back on him. I ran back and grabbed the part of the broken handle that was still attached to the wagon. When I turned the front wheels to one side the wagon stopped rolling.

I held up the portion of the handle I'd been pulling and burst out laughing. "No wonder this load felt so light!"

"It was light for you but not for me," Harry said. "I coulda been run over by a wagon!"

"But you weren't," I said. "It's a good thing we work together. Now we've got to figure out a way to get this wood home."

"I'm glad you know how to run things around here," Harry said.

"One day I'm going back to the life we knew in Marshall Village," I vowed. "This work is too hard!"

"Let's go get Vera, April and Gladys to help us," Harry suggested. "Barbara Jean will only get in our way."

"Great idea! Now you're talking, Bro. I'll stay with the wagon. Go get them and hurry back."

Harry picked up an armful of logs and headed up the path. I watched until I lost sight of him.

As Harry walked away, I shouted, "And don't leave me out here by myself too long. You know what Grandpa said about these woods."

"I'll be right back, Sis," he assured me.

To avoid hearing scary noises, I split up tree branches with the hatchet so they could fit inside the pot-bellied heater and the stove's top burner.

"Slinging an ax at trees is no fun, but it builds up muscles and makes me strong," I chanted repeatedly as the blade made the wood snap and crackle before it popped open. I felt my body relax when the woods came alive with the sound of running feet and children's voices. Soon a string of girls appeared, and it was my pleasure to stack logs across their outstretched little arms.

"I can take more!" Vera said. "I'm stronger than you think." I added logs until she grunted and said, "Now you can stop."

"Me too," April said. "One more. Try one more... Ugh! That's too heavy!" I removed the last log while Harry loaded his own arms.

"Just give me one more," Gladys said. "Stop! No more for me!"

Brave Harry led the way with Vera, April, and Gladys each bearing a comfortable armload of firewood in a beeline toward home. I trailed behind them so I wouldn't hold them up as I pulled the empty wagon with the broken handle.

When we got home, Harry finished the job of splitting logs by using a tree stump for a chopping block. He spit the logs into halves and fourths to make them easier to burn and to carry. After Vera and April stacked wood in the woodbin beside the kitchen stove, our work was done for that day.

* * *

That afternoon I left Harry outside spitting logs. Because my brother had trouble finishing what he started, I told him, "Finish the job first and then take a break." I went inside to get a drink of water and sat down for awhile before I went back outside. Harry was standing near the chopping block leaning on the ax handle. So I sneaked up behind him intending to surprise him with "Boo!" to remind him to get back to work. Just as I got near to him, Harry suddenly slung the ax over his shoulder and the rear corner of the steel ax-head hit me in the middle of my forehead.

"Ouch!" I screamed. Blood squirted from between my eyes like water from a garden hose. "I'm going to bleed to death!" I cried as I dashed back toward the house.

I ran inside screaming. Mama jumped up from her seat at the sewing machine faster than I'd ever seen her move before. She ran to the icebox and got some fatback, her usual remedy for cuts. She sliced a thick chunk of fatback and slapped it on my punctured forehead.

"This will stop infection," she said with such confidence that I believed I might live. "Hold it in place right here and be still for awhile," she said.

After a few minutes of sitting perfectly still, Mama removed the fatback and checked my forehead. The bleeding had stopped. She wiped my forehead, rubbed Blue Seal Vaseline Petroleum Jelly on the gash, and put two Band-Aids over the wound in crisscross fashion like an X. I felt branded and greasy for the next two days.

Did that accident cause me to lose my job of chopping down trees? Nope. Did Harry get a beating for hitting me in the head with an ax? Nope. Mama blamed me for getting hurt.

"Next time be more careful! You don't play around sharp objects," she said.

I wasn't even playing but I got the bad end of the stick. I learned that dangerous objects should be handled with care, used for their intended purpose, and stored out of reach of children. I also learned not to play a trick on somebody who's holding a dangerous object. I was so angry with Harry for not finishing his work before he took a break that I didn't say a word to him.

Later that night Harry sat down on the sofa beside me and whispered. "I'm sorry, Sis. I was just trying to show you I knew what to do without you reminding me. Now I know not to play when I have something in my hand that can hurt somebody."

"I'm glad to hear that," I said. He made me feel like getting hit in the head wasn't my fault. So I stopped being angry with him. Dang! I keep getting my feelings hurt when I try to do a good deed. "That's it! I'm not going to try to help anybody else," I murmured.

I woke up the next morning thinking about the kindling we had in the woodbin. I was grateful because one stick made a fire that quickly started the firewood burning that heated up the cold stove. I'll tell anybody that it's music to my ears to hear the truck driver's son yell, "Kindling! Twenty-five cents a bundle! Kindling!" I learned to wave my arms to flag down the delivery truck to buy another bundle of kindling before we ran out. Making a fire was so much easier with it.

As I walked to the kitchen I was thinking about how much harder it was to start a fire when I used rolled up paper instead of kindling. I had to stack thin hatchet-sliced pieces of wood in a crisscross fashion on top of the paper, and wait for the fire to start crackling before I could add thicker logs or chunks of coal to make it hotter.

It's easy to start a fire with kerosene too. We should keep a gallon of kerosene for starting fires only, I thought, even though the first time I made a fire with it I almost got my face burned off. Grandpa taught me well. I sure am glad I had enough sense to stand back. All I have to do is douse the wood, throw a match in the stove, and watch the fire blaze up and go "whoosh!"

I crossed my arms and rubbed my biceps while shivering from the morning cold. "That little kerosene heater doesn't do much to keep this house warm," I said to myself. I opened the door of the cold iron stove and started to make a real fire.

"It seems dumb that I've got to heat the stove so it can heat the pots before they heat the water," I was saying to myself as I walked to the woodbin beside the stove. When I leaned over to reach for a piece of kindling I noticed a thick rope neatly curled up in the seat of the old gray wicker chair beside the woodbin. I didn't recognize the thick red and beige rope. I assumed my sleeping brother, Harry, whose little bed was in the kitchen next to the chair, had put it there.

When I picked up the piece of kindling, I saw a snake's head raise up from the top of the rope. I was scared to death but I dared not scream. I didn't want to wake up the sleeping snake. I backed across the hardwood floor like a streak of lightning.

"SNAKE!" I shrieked, fleeing toward Mama's bedroom next to the living room. I banged on the door with both fists. "Mama, a snake is in our house!" I yelled. I glanced back and saw the raised head drop back down on the coiled up snake. Harry was rubbing his eyes as he began to sit up in bed. I'm sure he wondered why all the commotion.

"Don't move, Harry!" I whispered excitedly. "There's a snake by you!" I motioned with both hands for him to lie down, down, down. I pointed to the chair at the foot of his bed and put my index finger to my lips to tell him to be quiet. Then I turned and beat on Mama's locked door more frantically than before.

"Don't run to me!" Mama yelled from the other side of the door. "Go get Papa! I'm scared of snakes!"

I dashed out the front door and down the dirt path to get Grandpa Cox who usually supported his six-foot-four slender frame on a wooden cane. His one bad leg caused him to limp because of diabetes. I snatched open the front door that he never locked and yelled, "SNAKE! Hurry, Grandpa!"

Grandpa Cox kept a pair of trousers across the footboard of his bed but he already had on his trousers and union top when I barged in.

"I'm coming!" he shouted. He grabbed his cane and limped up the hill quickly as I trailed close behind him.

"It's in the kitchen chair next to Harry's bed!" I cried.

Grandpa Cox snatched the screen door open and then the wooden kitchen door. I saw the snake still coiled up in the chair. Wide-eyed Harry sat glued to his seat. He was speechless, as he stared at Grandpa Cox, our superman, who had come to save him.

"It's still in the chair Grandpa!" I yelled while standing safely outside.

Grandpa limped over to that chair and gave that snake a mighty whack with his wooden cane. The snake started to raise its head like it was mad at Grandpa for waking it up. That's when grandpa gave it another mighty whack and its head dropped down into the chair. Grandpa lifted the snake with his cane and headed for the back door. That's when I turned and shot around the house and ran inside through the front door.

Both Harry and I watched through the kitchen window as Grandpa took the dead snake down the path past the outhouse and buried it.

I ran outside to meet Grandpa when he came back up the path. "It won't bother you no mo," he said. "I done buried it in da woods where it come from."

"Oh, thank you, Grandpa," I cried as I hugged his waist.

As Grandpa limped back home, I ran back inside. I grabbed that gray chair and tossed it in the backyard. Then I chopped it up for firewood.

"Now I don't have to remember that snake or the memory of it coiled up in that chair," I said.

I replayed the entire incident over and over in my mind. "What if I had touched that snake? What if it had crawled in the bed with Harry? How did it get inside the house in the first place?

I started crying hard and couldn't stop as I thought about all that could have happened if Grandpa Cox hadn't come to our rescue.

I learned an important lesson that morning. Sometimes the people you run to in an emergency either cannot, or will not, help you. Mama didn't come out of her room, but my grandpa heard my cry and came to my rescue right away. I loved him even more after he killed that snake. I was so glad we could always depend on Grandpa Cox to be there for us.

"Grandpa will always be my hero," I shouted while tears rolled down my cheeks. "Even though Daddy's gone,

I still have somebody I can call on any time of the day or night and know that he will come when I call him."

That's when I realized that we moved to the country because Mama needed somebody she could depend on to help with her children now that Daddy was gone.

"Now I get it!" I cried. Harry didn't get a beating when he hit me in the head with the ax because Mama never beat us before. That was Daddy's job.

I finally understood that Grandpa Cox had taken on the job of teaching me how to survive country living because somebody had to do it. He trusted me to teach the younger ones so they could survive too. I promised him I'd do everything he taught me. *I will teach until I find a way to get out of this country and move back to the city,* I thought. I'm getting out of these woods if it's the last thing I do!

CHAPTER 8

"HELP! SOMEBODY HELP ME!" I cried as I wiggled to get away from the snakes crawling all over me. I leaped off the sofa bed. My knocking knees made a thumping sound as I made my way to the light. I fumbled around feeling for the light switch with one hand while pulling things off my face with the other.

"I've got to get them off of me!" I cried from the pressure inside my chest like a revving car engine. My whole body felt hot, sticky and wet with sweat. Something slid down my spine, so I reached back with both hands to pull that sliding creature off my back but my hands came up empty. I didn't want to see them but I had to get them off of me. I flicked on the light switch and glanced at the mirror on the wall. Then I looked down at the floor. I turned all the way around and saw nothing crawling.

"Where are the snakes I felt crawling all over me?" I asked. "Oh my goodness! Whew! Thank God it was only a dream!" I cried while staring at the bloody streaks on my cheeks. "I scratched my own face! That snake in the kitchen frightened me more than I thought. I've got to get out of this place! No! I'm getting out of this country if that's the last thing I do!"

I turned off the light and stumbled back to the sofa bed wondering how to make my escape. The last thing I remembered before I dozed off was imagining myself living with Lynette in Brooklyn, New York.

When I woke up, I had a stiff neck. My head was on the pillow and my feet were hanging on the floor. My first thoughts were, I start fifth grade next month. Where could I go? How could I escape without having a baby like my big sisters?

That afternoon, Uncle Clyde picked us up for a ride to Grandma Cox's oldest sister's house to celebrate her seventy-fifth birthday. When I climbed up the steps to Aunt Lula Bell's porch in her University Heights apartment I felt excited to be in the city again. I looked toward the street in front of her apartment when I heard a horn go, *"Beep, beep."*

A driver demonstrated his impatience with another driver who blocked traffic while trying to squeeze into a tiny parking space between two cars.

Uncle Clyde, who was walking in front of us, looked back toward the cars and laughed. "That person can't parallel park," he said. "They musta bought their license at Sears."

I jerked my head toward the busy traffic on Divine Street at the sound of *"SCREECH!"*

"Yup! Just as I thought." A female driver skidded to a stop at the red light just as an elderly woman inching along beneath a parasol crossed the street. The car's front bumper protruded into the crosswalk. I laughed when the elderly woman stopped right in front of the car, turned her head and shook her finger at the young driver. Then her jerky mini steps took her to the other side of the street. When the light turned green, the crowded city bus pulled away from the curb, leaving a trail of thick black smoke in the air. I coughed and turned to follow Mama inside the apartment.

The strong scent of undiluted Pine Sol greeted us at the door. The air outside is better than this, I thought. All the furniture was covered with thick clear plastic like it was being saved for use later on. I guess they're saving it for their next life, I thought. That's the only reason I could think of for having a plastic living room.

Aunt Lula Belle answered the door looking just like a full-blooded Cherokee Indian, complete with two long gray braids hanging over both shoulders with a rubber band on each end. A younger woman who resembled her sat nearby in a high-back wooden chair.

Aunt Lula Belle introduced her young twin. "Ya'll, everybody know my daughter Lucille?" She took baby steps in her thick-soled Hush Puppies over to Lucille and draped a colorful quilt over her legs. Aunt Lula Belle adjusted the quilt while Grandma Cox, Mama and Uncle Clyde set aluminum pans full of food on the kitchen table.

That's odd, I thought. I've never seen a mother take care of her grown daughter before. The grown daughter ought to be taking care of her old mother. As I faced the large picture window, I stared at Aunt Lucille out of the corner of my eye so I wouldn't be accused of gawking. I realized something was wrong when Aunt Lula Belle lifted Aunt Lucille's hand to adjust the quilt.

I peered out of the picture window and listened to the grownups talk about the car accident twelve years ago that left Aunt Lucille a paraplegic at forty years old. They talked about her son Willie in Washington, D.C. who never even came home to see his mother after the accident. They talked about the changes they've seen over the years as the University of South Carolina grew bigger and bought up all the property in downtown Columbia.

"We've come to celebrate a birthday," Uncle Clyde chimed in. "Let's sing to the birthday girl who is seventy-five years young today."

Mama led us in singing, *"Happy birthday to you, happy birthday to you, happy birthday dear auntie, happy birthday to you!"* We all clapped.

"She's your auntic but she's my big sister," Grandma Cox said in a mean way.

"Ohhhh," I chuckled, "Grandma spoke up that time."

"Well did you sing *happy birthday dear sister?*" Aunt Lula Belle asked.

"No 'cause I didn't wanna mess up the song," Grandma said. "Happy birthday, Sister! Now I feel better!"

Grandma could get sassy when she wants to, I thought, smiling. Aunt Lucille and Uncle Clyde were smiling too. Mama looked like her feelings were hurt. Sometimes grownups act like little children, I thought.

I could not believe my ears. Grandma talked more that day than I'd heard her talk the whole time we lived in the country. She and her only sister must have had fun growing up together. My family is too big for us to be close like that. I sighed.

"Everybody bow your heads right where you are," Uncle Clyde said.

I bowed my head and waited a moment before I heard his short grace, "God bless the food and bless the hands that prepared it. Amen. Now let's eat up all that food in the kitchen. All the children go last today."

I was firmly convinced that Aunt Lucille couldn't get up when she didn't move into the lineup. Mama fixed two plates and placed one on a food tray. Grandma Cox sat down beside Lucille and fed her food from the plate on the tray while she ate from the other plate.

I went to the kitchen and fixed myself a plate of fried chicken, potato salad, corn and cabbage and then went back in the living room to stand in front of the picture window to admire the scenery. I saw Booker T. Washington High School on my left and the University of South Carolina campus on my right. The flag of the United States, the state flag and a confederate flag flew on the dome on top of the Statehouse. I wondered why South Carolina needed two state flags while other states had only one.

As I watched the three flags flapping in the gentle breeze, I was thinking, *my aunts see flags on poles while we see trees outside our windows.* Then I heard a faint voice behind me.

"Take a good look, child," Aunt Lula Belle said, 'cause we'll be moving in a few weeks. The University bought all these apartments to put students in them. We moving 'cross town to Frazier Terrace."

When she mentioned moving across town I glanced over at Aunt Lucille who had been sitting in her high back chair in the same position all afternoon. I scooted over to the opposite side of the window.

"I'm so sorry," I said, "I've been standing here blocking your view."

"It's all right, I can see," she said.

I think she was glad to have someone talk to her rather than about her. *It must be a strange feeling to have hands that can't hold a fork and legs that can't move,* I thought. I wanted to ask her what her world was like being paralyzed but, of course, I dared not mention it. I wondered how Aunt Lucille got in the chair every morning and in bed at night, but I knew better than to ask that question too.

If Mama knew what I was thinking, she'd say, "All right, Davida, we came to celebrate Aunt Lula Belle's birthday, not to pry in Lucille's business."

My brother and sisters and I walked back and forth to the kitchen stuffing ourselves with food as the adults sat in the living room talking. As I sank my teeth into one of Mama's delicious sugar biscuits, my ears perked up when I heard Aunt Lula Belle say, "I need somebody to help me with Lucille 'cause I can't do it no more."

Words and crumbs shot out of my mouth before I knew it and I waved my arm. "I can help you take care of Aunt Lucille! Can I stay Mama? Huh? Huh?"

Uncle Clyde and all the women looked surprised. Grandma Cox's dark brown eyes twinkled as she stared at Mama. Mama seemed to read her mother's mind and slowly nodded her head a few times. After what seemed like an hour of silence, Mama looked around at everybody else, then looked straight at me.

"All right," she said.

"Thanks Mama! You won't be sorry!" I shouted.

I carefully placed my plate on the coffee table beneath the picture window. I ran over and hugged Mama until she pulled my arms from around her neck. I think she was shocked to see me so happy.

My thoughts raced ahead to move-in day. "May I look around?" I asked.

"You can but there ain't much to see," Aunt Lula Belle said.

"You got that right," Aunt Lucille chimed in with a smile.

I was happy to see her smile. I ran to the back door and opened it, only to see another row of apartments just like theirs. I saw a mop hanging over the metal banister on the back porch of the apartment directly behind us. Not much to see here, I thought. I grabbed a chicken drumstick as I ran past the kitchen counter then hurried through the living room toward the bedroom, and into the hall bathroom.

This will do just fine, I told myself. *The bathroom and kitchen have everything I need.*

When it was time to leave, I followed Grandma Cox out the door. Before Aunt Lula Belle closed the door behind us, I turned and ran back inside and kissed Aunt Lucille on her cheek. It was a pleasure to see her laugh.

"I'll be back soon," I whispered to Aunt Lula Belle as I walked out the door past her.

I started getting my clothes together as soon as we got home. I spent the next two days washing and ironing my clothes, especially my white cotton bras and panties. I had everything ready when Uncle Clyde came to pick me up after he got off work on Tuesday evening.

Uncle Clyde stopped his pickup in front of Aunt Lula Belle's apartment before dark and sat in the car with the motor running while I jumped out and ran to the porch to ring the doorbell. As soon as Aunt Lula Belle opened the door he honked his horn one time. I turned and saw him drive away as I walked through the door clutching my two big brown paper bags from Winn Dixie Supermarket in both hands. I was hoping no roaches had hitched a ride in my bags as I set them down on the floor next to the door. Then I walked over to stand in front of Aunt Lucille.

After she locked the door behind me, Aunt Lula Belle mumbled what sounded like, "I gotta finish washing the dirty dishes," and disappeared into the kitchen.

"Hello, I'm here to help," I said. The strong smell of Pine Sol tickled my throat and I coughed a couple of times.

"Thank you for coming," she said. "My slop jar's got to be emptied every night after I go to bed. Put enough water in it to cover the bottom and pour a capful of Pine Sol in it. A nurse's aide will come in around eight every morning and evening to help me get in and out of bed. You can use the wash basin to give me a sponge bath...." She talked a long time. After giving me my instructions she talked about how much she had enjoyed life before her car accident.

When the male nurse's aide showed up to put her in her twin bed, I stood back and watched him work. He was finished in no time and then he left.

On the first morning, I felt overwhelmed in my new home. "How am I going to remember to do all the things I have to do?" I asked myself but I made it through the first day.

That night I stretched out in a bathtub half full of warm soapy water with bubbles bursting all around me, and I remembered my bubble baths in Marshall Village. I cried for a moment. I think I cried because I felt comfortable, loved and special while my brother and sisters were still roughing it in the country. "I belong in a place like this." I declared to myself. "If Aunt Lula Belle could take care of her daughter, then I can too."

I slept on the sofa bed in my aunts' one-bedroom apartment in University Heights for three weeks as we packed boxes every day to prepare for our move to Frazier Terrace. Meanwhile, I kept my clothes in the two brown paper bags because it made no sense for me to unpack my things while packing theirs.

CHAPTER 9

UNCLE CLYDE and his oldest son Homer showed up around ten o'clock in the morning to move Aunt Lula Belle, Aunt Lucille and me to our new apartment. They walked in while two men were busy loading the moving van. Uncle Clyde shouted, "Hey, hey, hey! I like this."

I smiled when I saw how happy my uncle was to see the men at work.

Uncle Clyde and Homer stood around and watched the men move the furniture and heavy boxes. I stood on the front porch watching the movers until it was time to put Aunt Lucille in a special van that came to pick her up. Aunt Lula Belle and I rode in the van with Aunt Lucille to our new home in Frazier Terrace, leaving my uncle and cousin behind to clean up the old place.

I grabbed my aunt's chair and set it down on the sidewalk while I stared at our new home. I felt like a queen moving into a beautiful new palace as I stood admiring the stately columns in front of our brand new red brick two-story apartment in Frazier Terrace.

The driver got my attention when he asked, "Who's got the key?"

Clutching the chair, I ran down the sidewalk leading to the front door. I stuck my shiny new key that hung on a *Welcome* keychain into the keyhole. I opened the door, put the chair in the middle of the living room, then ran back to the van just in time to hear the driver telling Aunt Lucille, "I'm gonna move you on the count of three. Ready? One, two, three and lift." He lifted her onto a wheelchair and then pushed her to the front stoop. I ran ahead of them and held the screen door open for him. He pushed down on the handles and the front wheels hiked up in the air. He set the front wheels down on the stoop then pushed the wheelchair across the stoop of unit number B-7. He pushed down on the handles again and the front wheels popped over the front door's threshold. Then he lifted the handles and pushed the wheelchair inside the apartment.

I smiled as I watched the driver handle Aunt Lucille like she was precious cargo. Her grin from ear-to-ear proved that she enjoyed her ride. It must be fun to have a job that you like, I thought, as the van driver joked with Aunt Lucille.

"All right, Beautiful," he said, "this is the end of our ride together. Farewell, my love!"

"I don't mind if you stay awhile," Aunt Lucille told him as he wheeled her over to her chair.

"My wife might get mad if I stay too long," he said. "I'll have to take a rain check."

The driver leaned over and locked the wheelchair. Then he lifted her onto her favorite chair. "Plop," her body sounded when she connected with the leather seat.

"Thank you," Aunt Lucille shouted. She panted like she'd done some work herself.

"He's a nice man," I said as I helped Aunt Lucille get comfortable in her chair. "Oops," I said, while thinking, I should have pulled her frock up first. Oh well, I'll fix it later.

"Thank you, Sir," I told the van driver.

"I hope you ladies enjoy your new home," he said while leaving. I could hear him whistling "Dixie" as he pushed the wheelchair in front of him.

"He's a nice man," I said as I helped Aunt Lucille get comfortable in her chair.

"If I was twenty years younger and could cook I would've invited him to dinner," she said. "You know the second bedroom is all yours 'cause I can't get up them stairs."

"Really?" I cried. "I have a whole bedroom by myself."

I ran upstairs taking two steps at a time. First I ran into my empty bedroom and twirled around like a ballerina until I got dizzy. I found Aunt Lula Belle in the second bedroom bent over fluffing the pillows on her bed. I ran over and hugged her from behind. I startled her. I went in front and tried to grab her hands to waltz with her like I was dancing with Fred Astaire but she didn't cooperate. She lost her balance and plopped down on the side of her mattress, laughing.

"Oh my!" she exclaimed. "You're happy now!"

"You just don't know how happy!" I shouted. Tears welled up in my eyes.

I dashed over to the bathroom and talked to the skinny girl in the mirror. "Can you believe this? Here I am living in a spanking brand new apartment with a bedroom all to myself!"

I danced over to the bathtub and turned on the cold water and heard a gurgling sound like water finding its way through a maze. I waited until I saw clear running water. I held my hand beneath the faucet and wiggled my fingers as cold water ran through them. Then I turned on the hot water. I kept holding my hand beneath the faucet until I felt warm water.

"Ha! Ha!" I laughed.

I danced over to the commode and pressed the lever with my thumb. After hearing, *"whoosh,"* I watched water spin around in the toilet bowl on the way down and then begin to fill back up again. I could hear water pouring into the tank and the bowl was full again in no time. I heard *bloop* followed by silence from the water tank.

I held my head high and gracefully descended the stairs like a southern belle dressed for a ball. I twirled around and headed for the kitchen.

On the kitchen wall was a thermostat with a button for heat and one for air. I clicked the heat button first and heard a rumbling noise followed by air blowing from wall vents near the baseboards. While I waited for the heat I danced over to the stove and turned the knob to *High.* The burner soon turned red hot and I turned the knob to off. I felt the heat from the vents so I danced over to the thermostat to flick the button for air conditioning.

While waiting for cool air I opened the back door and saw nothing but pretty green grass that looked like it just sprang up a few days ago. I danced out back and did a little tap dance on the sidewalk and then danced back inside. The moment I came inside a cool breeze from the wall vent blew across my face!

"It works!" I cried out. "Everything works!"

"That's a good thing!" Aunt Lucille shouted back.

I'd forgotten all about anyone else being in the house. I laughed at myself as I opened the new refrigerator freezer door and saw nothing but two empty aluminum ice trays. The refrigerator was humming quietly as I filled the ice trays with water and returned them to the freezer. I knew Aunt Lula Belle would soon put lots of food in the refrigerator.

I danced back upstairs, this time taking one step at a time. I wanted to revisit the girl in the mirror to show her how pleased I was. She grinned at me like the Cheshire cat in Alice's Adventures in Wonderland. I knew exactly how she felt.

Next I ran down the stairs and out the front door. I saw lots of children playing outside in the Frazier Terrace playground next to the Community Room.

The first person I met was a skinny boy on a swing. He jumped out of the swing and walked right up to me. He stared at me and said, "You're new! I'm Gilbert. What's your name?"

"Hi. I'm Davida," I said. "We just moved in this morning."

To my surprise, Gilbert opened his mouth and hollered in my face, "Hey, everybody, c'mon over and meet the new girl!" Then he winked at me and said, "Tell 'em your name 'cause I forgot it already."

Gilbert stood beside me as lots of boys and girls rushed over and told me their names, too many for me to remember because they all spoke at the same time. After they ran back to the giant slide, swings, see saw and merry-go-round, I sat down in a leather-bottom swing and started pumping my legs.

Heaven must be like this! I thought, as I watched Gilbert swing so high that I thought he might flip over. "It's going to be fun living here," I mumbled.

By the first day of school I had lots of friends. It was so much fun walking and talking with them all along the sidewalk and across the railroad tracks to George Washington Carver Elementary. From the first ten-minute walk to school, every day brought a new thrilling adventure.

"Let's count every step we take and not tell anybody until we get to school," I suggested. "We should all have the same number. The one who messes up will lose a turn on the slide."

"That's a good idea," forgetful Gilbert said.

I'd counted fifty steps when Gilbert yelled, "I got fifty. Do everybody else got fifty?"

Nobody answered.

"Hush Gilbert! Just keep on counting," I shouted.

Everybody laughed.

Are they laughing at Gilbert's forgetfulness or because I told him to hush? I wondered. I smiled at my own boldness.

Gilbert's question wasn't so silly on the first cool morning that I wore my thin beige sweater – the only one I had.

"You ain't cold?" Gilbert asked.

"No!" I lied. I was too proud to admit that I was freezing.

A few minutes later as the chilly wind blew while crossing the railroad tracks, Gilbert asked me again, "Davida, ain't you cold?"

"I told you, no," I lied again.

When Gilbert asked me the same question on the third day, I decided to do something about it.

On Saturday morning I caught the bus to visit Daddy at his City Shed job.

"Daddy, I need a coat to wear to school," I said. "All I have is this beige sweater that the cold wind blows right through."

"Can you get a coat with two dollars?" he asked. "That's all I can spare today." He reached in his pocket and pulled out two one-dollar bills and handed them to me.

I was disappointed that Daddy didn't give me more money but at least I had something to spend.

"Thank you," I said. "See you next week." I ran and hopped on the bus headed toward Frazier Terrace and got off in front of K-Mart. I rushed over to the Girls' Department and found a rack full of coats. I slid the coat hangers, one-by-one, to examine each coat. A beautiful turquoise car coat with a zippered, white furry hood cried out to me, "I'm the one you're looking for!" I gazed at it for a moment then closed my eyes and wished I could afford it. I slowly turned over the price tag and read $14.99. Hmmmm, I thought. I took the car coat off the hanger and tried it on. It was a perfect fit. I hugged the coat and whispered to it, "You will be mine by Christmas!"

I took my dream coat to the register and put it on layaway, paying one dollar down. I imagined myself snuggled in it as I walked to school each morning feeling as snug as a bug in a rug. "I'll wear the hood of my beautiful coat flat on my back to show off the fur," I told myself. "But I'll wear it zipped up on real cold days to keep my ears warm."

I worked my plan by catching the bus almost every Saturday morning to go get money from Daddy. I hoped to get enough to get my coat out of layaway but he only gave me one or two dollars at a time. I paid fifty cents or a dollar on my layaway every week, but I didn't manage to pay it off before Christmas.

"What do you want for Christmas?" my aunts asked while we sat in the living room listening to Aunt Lucille's beloved Oral Roberts broadcast on Christmas Eve.

"A pair of skates and a pair of black and white saddle oxfords," I replied.

To my surprise, Aunt Lula Belle handed me two ten-dollar bills. "One's my present and the other one's from Lucille," she said.

I held up the money and danced in front of them singing, "Thank you, thank you, thank you!" I had more than enough money to buy both items and get my coat out of layaway. Unfortunately, they didn't give me the money until Christmas Eve. It was too late for me to make it to K-Mart.

I need a good plan for tomorrow, I thought. Suddenly, I knew exactly what to do.

I stayed in the house all day on Christmas. By not going outside I didn't have to explain to anyone that I didn't get any Christmas presents. When my friends knocked on the door, I didn't even answer. I kept the curtains closed all day. I watched the children skating along the sidewalk through the curtains but I made sure nobody could see inside. I spent a lot of time in the kitchen baking oatmeal raisin cookies and cleaning up my mess. That was a long day for me but I kept telling myself, "The day after Christmas is going to be a great day! Tomorrow will be my Christmas Day!"

Early the next morning I ran to the bus stop. I wanted to make sure nobody saw me. If they did, I wanted to appear like I was in too big a hurry to talk to them. I caught the bus downtown and was standing in front of K-Mart when the store opened. Everything in the store was on sale for much less than the cost before Christmas. I rushed straight over to the layaway desk.

"I want to get my coat off layaway," I told the cashier as I handed her my yellow ticket.

"Let's see," she said. "She looked in her little box and pulled out my layaway ticket. "You owe five dollars and fifty cents," she said.

I handed her a ten-dollar bill, she punched in some numbers on her cash register and a drawer popped open. She lifted a metal clip and put my ten-dollar bill in the drawer and then handed me four dollars and a fifty cents silver coin for my change. She counted my change aloud as she handed me each piece of money.

"That's $5.50, six dollars," she said after she handed me a fifty-cents coin, "seven, eight, nine, ten."

I'll save this for later, I thought as I tucked my money away in my change purse after the woman disappeared into a room behind the curtains. I looked around the store searching for the shoe department until I saw a big yellow sign that read, "Shoe Sale 50% Off."

"I'll go there next," I mumbled moments before the woman returned.

"Here you are," she said. "This is pretty coat."

I whirled around to see my coat. It was still wrapped in plastic. She took my coat off the hanger, placed it in a big shopping bag and handed it to me.

"Thank you," I said, resisting the urge to pull my new coat out of the bag and put it on. But as soon as I stepped away from the counter, I set my shopping bag down on the floor and pulled out my new coat. I hugged it against my breast. "Why not?" I said, then put it back in the bag and rushed over to the shoe department.

I removed my left shoe and placed my left foot on the long black metal foot-measuring device with the name Brannock on it. I stared down at the numbers and noticed that my big toe stopped at size six. Mr. Brannock must have had a real big foot, I thought.

Right then a red-haired salesgirl with freckles asked, "May I help you?"

"Does this mean I need to get a size six shoe?" I asked.

"You ought to get a half size larger to give your feet some growing room," she answered.

I hadn't thought about my feet growing some more. I learned something new. "Okay, I need a pair of black and white saddle oxfords size six and a half," I said, giggling.

"I'll be right back," she said.

I watched her go behind the counter and disappear in a stockroom. She returned with the shoes in a box while I was removing my right shoe. I put on the new pair of shoes and took a few steps in them. I looked at my feet in a mirror and liked what I saw. I flashed the salesgirl a big smile to show her the shoes fit my feet perfectly.

"Do you want to wear them?" she asked.

"Yes, I'd like that," I said cheerfully.

"Then step to the register and I'll ring you up," she said. I watched her put my old shoes in the new box and then followed her to the register.

My feet were laughing and I felt like dancing but I remained calm while I paid the sale price of four dollars and thirty-six cents for my saddle oxfords. I put the shoebox inside my shopping bag.

Next it was time to shop for roller skates. A big red sign announced SALE, ROLLER SKATES $2.49, WHILE SIZES LAST. I found a big stack of skate boxes on a table in the aisle.

"Please let them have my size," I prayed as I walked past larger sizes. Near the end of the table I saw size six on the box. I knew I could open skates and make them stretch up to size seven. It felt proud to know my correct shoe size. I grabbed my size and paid for them at the toy department register. I put them inside my shopping bag with my other purchases and walked out of K-Mart a very happy girl.

The moment I stepped outside K-Mart, I pulled my coat out of the bag and slowly put it on. I modeled in front of the store window to be sure it fit like I'd dreamed it would. It fit perfectly. People laughed at me as I admired myself in the store window but I didn't care. The coat was all mine. I left the tag hanging from the label and zipped up my new coat. I picked up my shopping bag by the handles and strolled to the bus stop. I felt beautiful, rich and warm.

I saw a bunch of kids outside skating in a line as I entered Frazier Terrace. I ran inside and tossed my shopping bag on my bed. I removed my new shoes and placed them on the closet floor. I put on my old pair of shoes and grabbed my roller skates. These skates aren't going to tear up my new shoes, I thought. After I tied the skate key to a long white shoelace and hung it around my neck, I ran outside in my beige sweater to join the other children on the sidewalks.

They'll see my new coat soon enough, I thought. I skated real fast to join the back of the skate train and caught Gilbert, of all people, by his waist. We skated all around Frazier Terrace like a choo-choo train.

"Davida, where was you on Christmas Day?" Gilbert had the nerve to ask me.

"Oh, I was at home. I couldn't come out yesterday," I answered truthfully.

This is my Christmas Day! I thought with a sheepish grin. This is how a child's Christmas is supposed to be. I felt like a normal child for a change and I loved it. I wondered why we didn't have sidewalks in the country. I took long strides, short strides, jumped over cracks in the sidewalk so I wouldn't break my mama's back, and skated backwards. After I had skated about ten laps around Frazier Terrace, my stomach growled and I knew it was time to eat.

When I walked through the front door with my skates on, warm air flowing through the vents hit my cool cheeks. I sat on the bottom step to remove my skates. In a few minutes I was warm all over. I ran upstairs to use the bathroom and came back down to prepare lunch for my aunts.

I fixed a quick lunch of Pork and Beans and wieners with cheese toast so I could go skate again. After I fed Aunt Lucille who seemed to eat slower than usual, I rushed back outside to skate another ten laps. I never wanted to stop skating. It's funny, but I didn't feel cold at all while I was skating, and I skated every day until the end of Christmas break.

* * *

As I dressed that morning, I muttered to myself. "This is the day I've been waiting for." It was our first day back at school. I had intentionally kept my car coat and new shoes clean because I wanted to surprise everybody. When I stepped outside to walk with my friends, all heads turned to admire the prettiest coat in the world.

"Girl, you sure wearing that color!" Gilbert blurted.

I smiled proudly and said, "Thank you."

When I strolled into my classroom, I saw my classmates turn green with envy at the sight of the prettiest coat in the school.

"See ya, wouldn't wanna be ya," I chanted in my brain while staring at the gaping mouths.

I knew how they felt because I knew what they said about other kids' clothes. But this time my coat topped all the rest.

"Wow! What a pretty coat!" students and teachers said all at once. "Was that a Christmas present?" several of them asked.

"Sure," I replied. There was no way I would tell them I bought it for myself.

"Who gave it to you?" asked Gilbert's nosey little sister, Melvina.

"My daddy," I proudly answered. I'd told the truth because most of the money had come from him, even though he hadn't seen the coat yet.

I wondered if anybody thought I didn't have a coat to wear before I got this one. Even though I had been ashamed to admit being cold, it seemed like somebody should have realized I was too proud to tell the truth.

"Oh well, I don't have to worry about being cold anymore," I declared to myself.

"I know you ain't cold no more in that coat," Gilbert told me as we walked home.

I didn't even bother to remind him that I never said I was cold. I thought it was strange that only forgetful Gilbert remembered I had worn the same sweater every day until I got my car coat.

When I got home, Aunt Lula Belle and Aunt Lucille both looked up from their seats as I walked through the door.

"Child, you lookin' pretty in your new coat!" Aunt Lucille said.

"You sure do," Aunt Lula Belle chimed in.

"I thank both of you," I said, as I strutted on inside. In that moment I made up my mind to wear my attention-grabbing car coat every day until the weather got warm. As a permanent member of the Frazier Terrace community, I felt like a rich girl. Life with my new family was fine, fun, and sometimes full of excitement.

CHAPTER 10

"RISE AND SHINE AND GIVE GOD GLORY!"
I shouted as I stood over Aunt Lucille who was stretched
out on her sofa bed. She lay awake waiting for me to help
her get up. I pulled off her quilt and lifted her heavy legs
one at a time over the edge of the sofa. Her legs were as
heavy as logs. Her feet were already covered with Bobby
socks to protect them from the cold tiled floor. With her
cheek resting against my cheek, I put my arms around her
torso and counted, "one, two, three and up" as I lifted her
to a sitting position.

"Ugh!" she grunted and gave a deep sigh. Rising from
lying flat on her back into a sitting position was a rough
journey for Aunt Lucille.

"Okay! I panted, "one more move. Ready?"

She nodded her head and braced herself for the next
move.

"One, two, three and up," I yelled, straining beneath
the weight of the heavy load of lifting her body into the
chair I had pushed against the sofa. We both grunted and
groaned a few times as she ended up in her resting spot
for the day. I was thinking, if anybody ever asks me how
she gets on that chair, I'll tell them, *She's heavier than an
armful of logs and a twenty-pound bag of coals. But with
God's help, we get the job done.*

As soon as I finished getting Aunt Lucille settled, I
made a mad dash upstairs to get ready for school. There
was no way I could afford to miss the morning walk with
everybody. I needed to hear what stupid things Gilbert
would say to jumpstart my day. He was so funny.

I walked into my fifth grade classroom while my
favorite teacher was placing textbooks on each desk. Mrs.
Collins pushed Mrs. Moss from first to second place as

my favorite teacher when she chose me to play the leading role of a dentist in the school play, *The Tooth, The Whole Tooth, and Nothing But The Tooth, So Help Me God.* I liked Mrs. Collins because she challenged her students to memorize long poems and songs in foreign languages like Frere Jacques and Au Clair de la Lune.

Memorizing was easy for me because I had my own bedroom with nobody to interrupt me when I studied. I'll never forget the night I recited the 23rd Psalm using my aunts as a live audience while I stood before them and practiced memorizing my lines. When I finished, Aunt Lula Belle must have clapped ten whole minutes while Aunt Lucille kept shouting the same words over and over again, "Hallelujah! Thank you Jesus! Amen!"

My goodness, they act like I just preached a great sermon, I thought.

Aunt Lula Belle waved her tiny fists in the air and yelled, "Yippee!"

"You done good!" Aunt Lucille shouted.

I thrived on the praises I got at home as well as those from Mrs. Collins at school. I especially liked to impress my teacher because she put cute little ink stamps on our papers and showered all her students with praises every day. She even thanked us for coming to school.

One day Mrs. Collins asked, "Who would like to volunteer to be the first reader of the new story in our textbook today?"

I automatically raised my hand. Sometimes Mrs. Collins called on a student who didn't raise his or her hand.

"Davida, begin reading *The Mighty Surrasuka* on page one hundred forty-six," she said.

I was surprised that she picked me out of all her students. Intrigued by the title, I flipped through the pages until I reached page one hundred forty-six. I was thinking, I'll show my teacher she made a wise choice by choosing me to be the first reader.

The moment I reached page one hundred forty-six and saw a huge snake coiled on the page with its head up and forked tongue stuck out at me, I screamed and hurled my textbook to the floor across the room. I wanted it as far away from me as possible. After a few tense moments of watching me tremble with fright, my classmates burst out laughing.

I got mad at them. They had no clue about my terrifying experience with a snake in my house. I sat in my seat sobbing and trembling. I couldn't make myself stop. I was thinking, I can't believe Mrs. Collins, of all people, set me up to make a fool of myself. As quickly as I had that thought, it vanished, because Mrs. Collins walked over to me, stood behind my seat, and gently placed both her hands on my shoulders to console me. Her touch was soothing to my frazzled nerves.

"Class," she said softly, "Don't laugh. We all have some things that frighten us. Davida happens to fear snakes. A fear is what we call a phobia. The morbid fear of snakes has been given the name ophidiophobia. Some people fear other things like falling, and heights, elevators, spiders, dogs, big crowds, and needles like the ones used to give you your school shots. Each phobia has its own name too."

Instantly the class stopped laughing! I could feel myself calming down. I was amazed that the teacher had spoken up for me. It felt good having a teacher who understood me. Tears streamed down my cheeks. The warm liquid that flowed from my eyes was a mixture of embarrassment for my actions, shame for exposing my fear, and joy for being made to feel special amongst classmates.

Nobody had ever hugged me and made me feel like I was somebody. I was amazed that Mrs. Collins' warm touch made me shiver. That one little touch meant so much to me.

I sat listening to other students read the story that I couldn't force myself to read because a snake was on every page. I kept thinking about ways to make Mrs. Collins proud of me.

After school that day, I skipped along the sidewalk wondering what would happen if I gently patted Aunt Lucille's paralyzed hand. I'll try it! I vowed.

I quietly entered the front door and then ran over to Aunt Lucille's chair while I had the courage to try something new. I patted her hand and leaned over and whispered, "I'm home!"

She raised her drooping head. I think she showed me all of her top and bottom teeth, all because of one touch.

"I like this!" I mumbled. "Now I understand how King Midas felt when whatever he touched turned to gold."

I decided to spread cheer in our home every day with a contagious touch. I ran upstairs and found Aunt Lula Belle resting on top of her bedspread. I shouted, "Hey, Aunt Lula Belle, let me touch you!" I gently stroked the flabby flesh on her thin arm and a broad smile showed her dentures.

"Let's touch every day," I said, "because a little touch goes a long way to brighten your day."

"Okay," Aunt Lula Belle answered. "Sounds good to me. I'll go downstairs and touch Lucille right now."

I watched Aunt Lula Belle grip the rail as she descended the six steps one by one. I shook my head as I observed her slow descent. It was obvious that climbing up and down stairs was a challenge for a senior citizen. I was happy to see her willing to try to make Aunt Lucille feel special even though both of them had to stay in the house all day long. The two of them were downstairs laughing while I changed into my play clothes.

"Yes! Thank you God," I said to myself. "Who says you can't teach an old dog new tricks?" I laughed and looked up at the ceiling. "God, you know I wasn't calling my aunts *old dogs!*" I whispered so only God would hear me.

After I took off my school clothes, I ran downstairs to cook dinner. I remembered my comment about teaching old dogs new tricks, and then I thought about the new Bible classes in the Community Room starting at six o'clock. I had to finish dinner early because I really wanted to go.

"Don't put no meat in my greens," Aunt Lucille, the Seventh Day Adventist, shouted from the living room. "Don't put no fatback or lard in none of my food."

"I want you to fry the fatback and pour the grease in my greens," Aunt Lula Belle, the Baptist quickly said. She was quiet about most things but spoke up about her food. "Food ain't worth eating if it don't have no flavor," she said.

It didn't take a long time before I figured out that it was easier for me to cook collard greens, or whatever, without meat in one pot and then add seasoning later after I removed Aunt Lucille's unseasoned portion. After I prepared the meal and we ate, I was free to do my homework in peace, go play outside, read a book silently or read aloud to my aunts. One simple cooking lesson taught me how to work smart and "kill two birds with one stone," as Mama said, to stop the food arguments between my aunts.

Nobody visited our house except Aunt Lucille's doctor who came one time in October carrying a big black medicine bag. My aunts usually spent all day – everyday – inside the house listening to a floor model Victrola. At first, it was a challenge for me to learn how to place the needle on the edge of a 78 RPM as it spun around and around on the turntable. But after I learned to look for the grooves in the record that challenge disappeared.

My heart fluttered every time one of my aunts said, "Thank you. I'm so glad you're here to help us." They made me feel like I made a wise decision in coming to live with them.

I sat across from Aunt Lula Belle at the shiny chrome dinette table with floral seat cushions as we ate the food seasoned with pork. I could count on her to sprinkle extra black pepper on almost everything she ate. At the same time she could count on me to start sneezing before she put the shaker down. Her dentures didn't hinder her at all from enjoying every bit of her food. She also lapped up every word I said about my day at school.

"Tell me more! And then what happened next? Tell me all about it and don't leave nothing out."

Sometimes I felt uncomfortable when she stared at me through a gray film like Saran Wrap that covered her weak eyes as she held on to every syllable. She acted just as excited as my little sisters the first time I read them the Cinderella story.

Occasionally, Aunt Lucille chimed in as I talked. She mainly concentrated on slowly chewing the morsel of food that I fed her every few minutes. After she swallowed her food she always sipped some drink through a long straw "to wash it down." I could talk for a long time before she would say, "I'm ready for another bite."

After dinner, Aunt Lula Belle talked about Jesus while we stood at the kitchen sink washing dishes. "My merciful Savior gave me one more day in the land of the living and I thank him," she said. "I'm living on borrowed time."

I listened with awe about the borrowed time bit. She had explained it once before but I forgot it or didn't understand it, so I just accepted that she wasn't supposed to still be alive at age seventy-five, but she was.

Maybe she's been around so long that God forgot about her, I thought.

"Wonderful Jesus!" Aunt Lula Belle said over and over again for no special reason. She babbled on and on about her merciful Savior as she washed dirty dishes and rinsed them beneath running water. I dried the dishes and put them away.

"Washing dishes in this house is more like having fun than working because I have a partner to help me," I told Aunt Lula Belle. "I'll wash the pots and pans after they soak awhile." The scorched tomato paste on top of my meatloaf baked into the Pyrex dish. I knew not to leave dishes soaking overnight.

Aunt Lula Belle reminded me for the thousandth time of the importance of washing all the dishes. "We can't leave one dirty dish overnight or the roaches will come in here. All it takes is one roach to come in and find a crumb. He goes back and brings A-L-L his kin folks and they come and take over the house and even Raid can't get rid of 'em."

Suddenly I glanced at the clock that read 5:48. "Aunt Lula Belle, I almost forgot! I've got to hurry down to Frazier Community Room for Bible Study with the missionaries tonight!" I folded the dishtowel and hung it over the bottom of the three-tier towel rack on the wall. I patted her on one cheek and whispered, "I promise I'll finish the dishes as soon as I get back!"

I rushed out the front door and ran all the way down the sidewalk so I wouldn't be late. The first thing I saw was a group of white college students, who called themselves missionaries. The poster said they had come to recruit students for a week of Bible school. It was starting tonight. I was excited about their promise to serve cookies and Kool-Aid and give us a perfect attendance certificate at the end of the week if we would come out every night.

It was fun being packed in the community room like sardines in a can from six o'clock until seven-thirty. Almost everybody sat on the cold tiled floor with their legs crossed, Indian style. A few or us stood against the wall. I stood up the whole time, first of all, because I was one of the last to arrive, and also because I never learned how to sit with my legs crossed beneath me. I didn't want anybody to know that I couldn't make my legs stay crossed and be comfortable.

It looks so easy, I thought, as other children and even the missionaries slide into position on the floor. I felt bad because I knew I couldn't cross my legs like that.

The missionaries taught us the names of all the books of the Bible, fun Christian songs like *Jesus Loves Me, If You're Happy and You Know It, Let the Sunshine In,* and my favorite, *Father Abraham*. Chris, the tall leader of the group with green eyes, kept leading us in a chant after every song: "I believe in Jesus and I pray; I trust in Him and I obey." That first night we repeated the same words so often that most of us memorized what we needed to know for the rest of the week.

After the last song, Chris pointed at us with both index fingers. Instantly, there was a thunderous response from the crowd, "I believe in Jesus and I pray; I trust in Him and I obey."

Chris and the other four missionaries clapped for us and shouted, "Hallelujah! You kids are awesome!"

Next we played a game of "Jesus Says." In this game we only did what Jesus told us to do. It was easy and fun for me because I was already good at playing "Simon Says."

"Jesus says, sing a song," a missionary commanded and everyone began to sing.

"Jesus says, hop on one foot," another missionary commanded and we hopped.

"Jesus says, shout Amen!" a third missionary commanded and we shouted.

The commands came faster and faster and I did whatever the missionaries commanded us to do until Becky suddenly yelled, "Name the first book of the New Testament!"

Most of the children shouted "Matthew," but I didn't open my mouth because she hadn't said, Jesus says....

Chris noticed that I didn't answer so he pointed at me and yelled, "Come on down front!" Becky ran over to escort me to the front of the crowd. I'm sure my face lit up like the sun as I beamed with pride. Someone had noticed me out of all the children in the room. Chris patiently adjusted a shiny gold cardboard crown and leaned over to place it on my head.

"I cried earlier today in my class at school, but tonight I'm laughing in this class," I whispered as he crowned me. "Thank you for making this a good day after all."

"You're very welcome," he said, smiling. "What's your name?"

"Davida," I answered.

"Davida, turn around and face the crowd," he said.

I turned around and he touched my crown. "Davida is the winner of our first OCOG Award," he said real loud like it was important.

"OCOG Award???" I stared into a sea of confused faces. I didn't care what OCOG meant because I knew it was something good.

"Yeah, don't you get it?" Chris asked the question like we should already know what it meant. "She's our first Obedient Child of God!"

I could tell by the way he glanced over at the other missionaries that he had just made up that name. They all looked at each other and laughed, then shouted, "Oh yeah!" like they knew what it meant all along. I laughed along with everybody else who realized that he made up that name on the spot.

Chris reached down and raised my right hand and announced, "Here's tonight's winner of the Obedient Child of God Award. Everybody stared at me and clapped. When the clapping subsided he said, "Tomorrow night it could be you!" Chris looked around. "God hears and answers prayers. God wants us to ask him for things because he owns everything, but we still must do our part. Remember, you can't win if you don't come back and play *Jesus Says*."

As I returned to my spot along the wall I felt confident that I'd already learned the lesson he was teaching because I prayed for a pretty car coat for Christmas, but I was the one who shopped for it, put it on layaway and made payments until it was mine.

I was determined not to miss a night. I went home and washed the soaking dishes so Aunt Lula Belle could see that she could trust me to keep my word. She sat listening to me describe how I had won the OCOG Award while I washed dishes with help from the Brillo pad, while still wearing my golden crown. That was the first night of fun at Bible School.

Around six o'clock the next morning, I asked Aunt Lucille, "All right, are you ready to rise and shine?"

"I'm ready," she giggled.

She seemed as eager to get up as a hungry baby searching for the nipple on a bottle of milk.

"Ready?" I asked. As soon as she nodded her head, I counted, "one, two, three and up!"

She laughed as usual when I wrapped my skinny arms around her. As I lifted her off the sofa bed on the count of three she didn't seem as heavy as usual. I didn't even grunt when I sat her paralyzed body on the wooden chair with a round hole cut in the seat.

"The missionaries told the truth when they taught us to say, 'I can do all things through Christ that strengthens me'," I told myself. From now on I'm just going to have fun moving her and not even think about how heavy she is.

I slid the night pot beneath the hole in the seat bottom after I added a capful of Pine Sol to the fresh water. Lifting twenty-pound bags of coal and loads of firewood while living in the country had made me strong enough for this job. But I found it hard to imagine how Aunt Lucille felt not being able to walk any more. It's so sad that all she can do is sit upright in that chair and think about how her life used to be before the car accident, I thought.

"It's nice for people to have relatives they can visit," I whispered to Aunt Lucille. "I just love living here in Frazier Terrace."

"It was boring just being here with mama all day long before you came," she said. "Young people add life to dead situations."

I laughed. She made me feel like my being there was good for them.

Every evening that week I finished all my cooking and chores early so I could go to Bible School. Then on Friday night it was time to say goodbye to the missionaries.

"May I hug you?" I asked Chris after class.

"You betcha!" he said, grinning. "We want a hug from everybody so line up behind Davida!" he said.

I grinned from ear-to-ear as I wrapped my arms around him while standing on my tippy toes. He hugged me too. Then I went down the row and hugged each of the missionaries and they hugged me back. I don't remember ever being hugged like that before. It felt great! I cried as I walked back to our apartment after saying goodbye. I didn't want the fun to end. I marveled at tonight's closing events as I floated home carrying my perfect attendance certificate in one hand and nibbling on my special treat in the other hand, a yummy ice cream sandwich.

Bible school called for a change in my daily routine. Living with elderly relatives in Frazier Terrace had made me more astute at handling adult responsibilities and solving real-life problems. But I liked the good feeling I got from playing fun games with other children and learning new things that we didn't study in Mrs. Collins' class. I also liked the coconut and lemon cookies and Kool-Aid the missionaries served us every night.

After our nightly count to three, I put Aunt Lucille down on the sofa bed so she could get her final touch before going to sleep. I was surprised to hear what she said that Friday night.

"I'm sorry you have to work so hard," she said softly. "I know I'm a lot of trouble."

"It's much easier to carry a slop jar upstairs to the bathroom than to carry it down a path to the outhouse in the cold and rain," I told her. "Besides, you aren't heavy, you're my auntie."

She laughed as I tucked a homemade quilt around her neck. "You know what I'm talking 'bout," she said with a sober look on her face that I ignored.

Lifting her was part of the reason I had come to live with them. I was willing and able to do whatever they needed done around the house, and I never complained. I was content with my new life until that day in April when Doctor Howard paid Aunt Lucille another visit.

CHAPTER 11

"HOW DO YOU SPEND YOUR DAYS?" Doctor Howard asked Aunt Lucille as he pressed a flat round metal disk on her chest and back. She jerked each time he moved it.

"That thing is cold!" Aunt Lucille cried out.

Aunt Lula Belle and I sat at the dinette table and watched as the doctor examined her with the other end of the stethoscope stuck in his ears. I wondered how he could hear her answer his questions if he was busy listening to her heart with his ears plugged up.

"Sitting in my chair and listening to the radio," Aunt Lucille answered. "I always have Davida put my hands on the radio when Oral Roberts come on. He's a ler, you know. Are you a Christian?"

The doctor turned to me and asked, "How old are you?"

"Eleven," I answered, wondering why he wanted to know how old I am? He's here to check Aunt Lucille, not me, I thought.

"An eleven-year old girl has no business lifting a hundred-and-fifty-pound woman twice a day," the doctor said to Aunt Lula Belle. "She'll probably experience back pains for the rest of her life if she continues lifting dead weight. Lucille needs a man to lift her."

He's got his nerve! I shot back in my mind. It's April and I've been lifting her ever since I came to live with them last August and I never once let her fall. He didn't even ask me to show him how I lift her. Yeah, it was hard at first but now it's just fine.

Aunt Lula Belle, knowing she couldn't lift Aunt Lucille at all, said softly, "I'll see if we can get Lucille's son to come down from Washington, D.C. and help us. But we don't hear from him much."

"You need to contact him sooner rather than later," Doctor Howard said real mean to Aunt Lucille, shaking his head like he was disgusted. He packed his stethoscope in his big black leather bag and snapped it shut. Finally, he said, "That's the doctor's order!"

I stood at the door waiting to close it behind Doctor Howard. He was the first doctor I'd ever seen making a house call. Before he crossed the threshold he stopped and spoke softly to me as if to prevent my aunts from hearing him.

"You're a strong girl. I'm amazed at what you do for your aunt. But a move would be for your own good," he said as he walked out the door.

"Thank you, sir," I said. The doctor's kind words to me made me feel a little bit better because I didn't like the way he talked to Aunt Lula Belle. As I closed the door quietly after he left, I felt sorry for Aunt Lula Belle and her daughter who had lived together for so many years. I could hear them discussing how they thought Willie might feel about helping them out. While they were talking I began to dread going back to live in the country.

The very next day Aunt Lula Belle called Aunt Lucille's son and told him his mother needed his help. When she hung up the phone she turned to Aunt Lucille and said, "Willie promised to think about it." I could tell that he had given them hope.

Three days later, Willie called back. Rather than moving into Frazier Terrace with them, he promised to come to Columbia when my school year ended in June and move them to Washington, D.C. to live with him.

Aunt Lula Belle smiled. "Willie done got our kin folk up north to agree to help him take care of us," she said.

"I ain't seen my son in years," Aunt Lucille said.

That was a happy day for Aunt Lucille. The closer it got to June, the more excited she became. She seemed to be more thrilled at the thought of seeing her son again than going to live with him.

How could a child, especially an only child, go away and never come home to visit his sick mother? I asked myself. I don't understand how that could happen. The thought brought to mind my baby sister, Sulema. I tried to imagine how she must feel being separated from her family through no fault of her own. So I decided it would be a good idea if Sulema and I both went home together.

* * *

That Saturday morning, I caught the bus to the City Shed to tell Daddy about Mama giving Sulema to the old gray-haired couple who lived in Marshall Village. As soon as he walked off the yard I called out to him.

"Daddy, please go get Sulema and bring her back home to live with everybody else," I begged.

"That's your Mama's baby and she can do what she wants with her," he barked.

I was shocked! Daddy's answer destroyed all my hopes of getting somebody to force Mama to take her baby back. I felt defeated in trying to keep my family together. At least I tried to help Sulema out as I walked away sad, with my head hung down and my shoulders drooped. I felt like I was carrying a ton of bricks on my back.

* * *

Back at home in Frazier Terrace I helped my aunts decide which things to keep and which they should give away. We all agreed they'd keep all their odds and ends, picture albums, the big white Holy Bible, clothes, quilts and other keepsakes. Aunt Lucille would keep her chair with the hole in the seat. They would donate all the other furniture to the Salvation Army.

Even though I felt like a failure in my attempts to keep my family together, I felt like a champion when I finished my fifth grade year with all *A*s on my report card. During the year I lived with my aunts, I knew for sure that

I had learned many important things, one of which was that God made me somebody special.

Dang! I'm going to miss this place, I thought. I sat at the kitchen table our last night together, thinking about all the things I liked about living in Frazier Terrace. Unlike Marshall Village with scary Creepy Crater, Frazier Terrace had a paved street running through the center of the buildings and brand new sidewalks all around it. I liked the streetlights that made me feel safe while outdoors at night. I was thinking, this year I've become a champion roller skater, a fast reader, a good cook, a patient nurse to Mama's cousin, a good friend to an elderly aunt, a happy child who knows how to make work fun, and an excited Bible student.

The sound of a noisy truck interrupted my thoughts. The driver pulled up and stopped in front of our apartment. I glanced out the picture window and saw a U-Haul truck. A tall, slim, handsome man jumped out of the driver's seat and walked around the front of the truck and onto the sidewalk leading to our front door.

"It's Willie just like he said!" Aunt Lucille shouted. "My child's come home."

Willie was reaching for the doorbell when I opened the door. He laughed. "You beat me to the punch. You must be Davida." He patted the top of my head. I liked him right away.

"Yes sir," I said, smiling. "Willie's here, Aunt Lula Belle!"

"Aunt Lula Belle went upstairs to rest after dinner," I told him.

Right away, I heard her grunting as she came down the stairs. I think we all wondered whether or not Willie would show up like he promised. I was delighted that he had not disappointed them.

Willie strutted into the house singing Pearl Bailey's song real loud, "*Won't You Come Home Bill Bailey, Won't You Come Home? She moans the whole day long. I'll do the cooking darling, I'll pay the rent; I knows I've done you wrong."* His singing stirred up excitement.

"Willie, is that really you?" Aunt Lula Belle shouted while slowly descending the steps.

"It's me, live and in living color, standing just as tall as ever," he joked.

Willie waited at the bottom of the steps to meet her. He wrapped his long arms around his wee little grandma, practically smothering her. "Yep, it's your long-lost grandson. It's so good to see you."

"Thank you for coming," Aunt Lula Belle said after he released her.

"I had to," he said. "I couldn't let you ladies down. Besides, it was just plain ole time to come see my two favorite people."

He turned and took one look at his mother seated in her chair and rushed over and plopped down on the sofa beside her. He took one of her hands in his. "Ma, what took you so long to call me?"

"I didn't want to be a burden to you, son," Aunt Lucille choked on her words.

"I'm your son, Ma," he said. "Grandma is too old to take care of you and Davida is too young. The doctor was right. From now on, I'm gonna take good care of you!" He slapped one hand on his thigh and declared, "Yep! That's what I'm gonna do!"

"Okay!" she giggled like a schoolgirl. "I'm so glad to see you at last."

Willie gently laid her hand down on her lap, then walked into the kitchen. I watched him out of the corner of my eye from my seat at the dinette table. He removed a long skinny raggedy-looking cigarette from his shirt pocket that looked quite different from Daddy's perfectly round Winstons. After patting his pant pockets a time or two looking for matches, he turned on the kitchen stove and leaned down to light the funny-looking cigarette hanging from his mouth. Without saying a word he went out the back door and smoked for a long time.

I could clearly see Willie's silhouette through the

curtains because the streetlight was directly behind our house above the two rows of garbage cans for our building. After awhile, I got up and went upstairs because I started thinking about all the times I'd watched my Daddy smoke in front of us, especially before story time.

I was still missing my daddy. I followed Aunt Lula Belle upstairs, where she was already dressed in her long cotton nightgown and was combing her shoulder-length gray hair as she stood in front of the bathroom mirror. I heard the back door shut while I fluffed the extra pillow on my bed for Aunt Lula Belle to rest her head. In her long pigtails, Grandma Cox's sister looked just like their Cherokee papa in the photograph in the mahogany picture frame on the dresser.

"Which side do you want to sleep on?" I asked. Aunt Lula Belle had given her bedroom to Willie for the night.

"Child, it don't matter," she said. "I'm just glad the good Lord blessed me with my own bed all these years. No telling where we gonna sleep in Washington."

She sounded scared about going to Washington. "It'll be all right, Auntie," I said, "God will take care of you wherever you go."

"I know child, I know," she said, "I just always had my own house." She leaned back in bed on her right side as I stared into her face. She sounded tired and worn out. As soon as her head hit the pillow she started snoring. I gave her a light kiss on her forehead then ran down the steps to check on Aunt Lucille.

"It's time for our one-two-three," I announced in front of Willie.

"Let me do the honors tonight," he said.

I felt embarrassed for Aunt Lucille when her son took off her dress and put her gown over her head. He wasn't gentle with her at all. He lifted her to the sofa with no help from her whatsoever.

"I wasn't ready yet!" she complained after he whirled her onto the sofa.

"Oh, then next time tell me when you're ready," he said.

I grabbed the night pot and ran upstairs to empty it and put fresh water and a bottle capful of Pine Sol in it for the last time. I carried the pot back downstairs and slid it beneath the chair. I felt good about having shown Willie everything he must do before putting Aunt Lucille to bed.

"Goodnight," I said, pulling her quilt up around her neck. I bent down to kiss her forehead. "I love you," I whispered, then stood up, and turned to Willie who was sitting at the dinette table engrossed in reading the centerfold of a Jet magazine. I waved goodnight to Willie so I wouldn't interrupt him and ran upstairs to end the long night.

The next morning, on the last day of school, Willie was still asleep in Aunt Lula Belle's room when I got Aunt Lucille up. I fought back tears at the thought of my aunts moving away. At school my tears flowed as I bid my friends and my beloved teacher, Mrs. Collins, goodbye. I was losing everybody and it felt like a dagger was piercing my heart.

Mrs. Collins asked the class, "How will you spend your summer break?"

When it was my turn I said, "I've got to go back home because my aunts are moving to Washington, D.C." I was careful not to tell them the real reason why they had to move.

Mrs. Collins stroked my ego one last time. "Oh Davida, I'm sorry to hear that. But I expect great things from you wherever you are."

Unfortunately, her words made me cry rather than smile. Moving always meant never seeing my friends again.

When I returned home that afternoon, I saw stacks of boxes in the living room that Willie and Aunt Lula Belle had packed. There was a big pile of furnishings that Willie had decided they didn't need any more. Whenever Aunt Lucille mentioned something she wanted such as her favorite lamp when she was a child, an old wooden musical jewelry box, and a black cast iron skillet, Willie

would say, "Trash it," or "Give it to somebody," or "I'll
get you another one." That conversation went on and on
until Uncle Clyde showed up to drive me home.

"Take whatever you want," Willie told Uncle Clyde
and me. I picked up a stack of 78 phonograph records.
These will make great flying saucers, I thought. At least
my little sisters can have some new toys to play with.
They'll like the toys but they won't like it when I take
back my sofa bed.

"Remember the doctor's orders, Davida," I muttered
to myself as I remembered all the comforts I was giving
up by leaving Frazier Terrace. I hadn't seen my family for
a whole ten months and I wondered what had changed at
home and whether or not my little sisters would remember
me. I took a big box containing odds and ends plus my
clothes, shoes, and 78 records. I put them on the back of
Uncle Clyde's pickup truck.

Uncle Clyde helped Willie load some boxes on the
U-Haul as I finished gathering my things. I had a lot more
than to carry than the two brown paper bags of clothes I
had brought with me last August.

I gave the magic touch to Aunt Lula Belle first and
then to Aunt Lucille. Suddenly I realized that a touch
wasn't enough, so I hugged their necks for a long time.

"I'm sorry to see you go," I cried. "Thank both of you
for being my mama all year long. I'll never forget you as
long as I live."

Aunt Lula Belle reached in the pocket of her housecoat
and pulled out a handkerchief covered with daisies. When
she dabbed at the corner of her eyes with it, I wept.

Aunt Lucille cried real hard as I walked toward the
door. I felt like I was losing two people who loved me and
I couldn't do a thing about it. It was the doctor's orders.
For some reason, I felt like I would never see them again.

"Willie, remember 'one-two-three' will make your
Mama laugh when you pick her up and put her down," I
yelled as I headed to the pickup where Uncle Clyde was

impatiently honking the horn. I think he went outside because he was about to cry too.

As we rode home in silence I wondered what would become of my aunts now that it was Willie's turn to take care of them. I thought about having to deal with babies, bedbugs and Mama's boyfriend, Mr. Fred. I had my own problems ahead of me, some I knew about, and some I didn't.

CHAPTER 12

AS SOON AS UNCLE CLYDE'S TRUCK turned into our dirt driveway in the country, familiar heads bobbed in the dusk as little children raced toward us. When the truck stopped, I jumped out and began hugging the welcoming committee – my little sisters.

"You're back, you're back!" Vera shouted. Vera, April, and Gladys hugged me at the same time.

"I'm glad you girls didn't forget me," I said with tears in my eyes. They'd gotten much bigger in ten months. I noticed Barbara Jean trailing after the others, running sideways with uncertain steps. She looked sad because she couldn't keep up with the pack. I broke away from the others and ran to hug Barbara Jean so she would feel special. Her smile was priceless. Uncle Clyde gave my things to Vera and April who walked sideways as they struggled beneath the weight of the heavy box. Gladys ran ahead to the front porch while I walked along slowly, holding Barbara Jean's hand.

"Surprise!" Gladys yelled when I entered the house. I stopped in my tracks at the sight of a baby in a pink blanket lying on the sofa. I stared at the tiny bundle in disbelief.

"That's Carrie, our new baby sister," Gladys said.

I pretended I didn't see that baby. I walked on toward the kitchen and into the bedroom to see if anything else had changed. "Dang! Nothing's new but that baby!" I murmured.

Oh well, it was a nice thought anyway. I pictured myself back at my old job of boiling water to make glass bottles of Carnation formula for Carrie Cox, a tiny premature baby whose last name was the same as Mama's maiden name.

"Why is Carrie's last name Cox and not Kincaid like all the rest of us?" I asked Mama.

"'Cause I was mad at my husband, that's why!" Mama snapped.

Mama's swift attack made me feel like a roach about to be crushed by a shoe. I wanted to run for cover but there was no place to hide. This was home and I was the eldest child – Mama's helper returning to active duty. I don't know who helped Mama while I was gone but life was the same as usual after I returned. How I longed for Frazier Terrace.

* * *

Three weeks after coming home from Frazier Terrace, it was the day before the fourth of July and I was outside playing kickball. Suddenly, I felt wet – like I had peed on myself.

"Time out!" I yelled. I quickly ran into our bedroom to check out my panties and discovered bloodstains. I changed my panties, washed them with cold water, hung them on the clothesline outside, and resumed my position at home base.

A few minutes later, I felt wet again. This time I was concerned about interrupting my game. I ran back inside.

What's going on? I wondered.

I pulled my yellow shorts and panties down and saw blood again. Then I looked up and saw Mama standing in the half-opened bedroom doorway staring at me. She didn't say a word.

"I don't know what's wrong with me, Mama. I'm bleeding." I know I sounded confused because I was. "I must have kicked the ball too hard and hurt myself."

"I know what it is," Mama said. "You're gonna have a baby."

"A Baby! I don't want a baby!" I protested. "I just want to have fun playing kickball!"

Mama stepped into the bedroom and closed the door behind her. She reached into the chifforobe and handed me a sanitary belt and a napkin from a Kotex box. "You have to wear this napkin to catch the blood," she said. She opened the clasp on the elastic belt and showed me how to fasten it around my waist. "Be sure to wrap the gauze over the hook on both ends," she said. "You want the napkin to stay in one place when you put it between your legs."

I did what Mama said but I didn't catch on right away. My hands trembled and I started praying, "Please God, I don't want to have a baby. We already have enough babies around here." Tears blurred my vision.

Mama grabbed the back end of the napkin and showed me just what she was talking about. She fastened the napkin over a hook.

"Now I'll leave you to fasten the front just like that after you put the belt 'round your waist," she said.

After Mama walked out of the room and closed the door behind her, I pulled the end of the thick napkin through the hole in the sanitary belt and hooked it like she did. When I stood up straight, I felt like I was wearing a baby diaper between my legs.

"This can't be real!" I told myself as I paced the bedroom floor. Finally, I got the nerve to go back outside. I was hoping nobody would notice the bulky napkin between my legs. I was worried that everybody would find out that I was going to have a baby.

"Are you ready for your turn?" April asked as soon as she saw me.

"Naw, go on and play without me," I replied. "I don't feel like playing anymore."

Wearing that napkin spoiled everything. While everybody else was running and playing, I tried to keep still so the bleeding would stop. But it didn't. I bled for several days and had to keep changing the napkin. I wrapped the soiled napkins in newspaper and tossed them in the outdoor toilet. After five days the bleeding wasn't as heavy as it was it first. Then on the sixth day there was only some brown spots on the napkin. On the seventh day, when there was only one more napkin left in the box, I told Mama, "I'm not bleeding anymore."

"That's about right," Mama said. "You can stop wearing the napkin after about seven days."

With the pad removed, I felt like a prisoner stepping outside prison walls for the first time in years. I was so glad the baby didn't come while I was wearing the napkin. I enjoyed my freedom and had lots of fun with my little sisters and brother for the next few weeks. But the first week in August, I got another wet surprise while competing in a Hula Hoop contest. I ran inside and saw Mama sitting at the sewing machine.

"Mama, I'm bleeding again, just like the other time."

Mama looked up and said. "You gotta keep a calendar and count every 28 days 'cause it's gonna keep on coming back 'til you have a baby. I didn't get my monthly till I was thirteen years old."

"I'm only eleven," I said. I felt like I'd done something very bad to get my monthly two years earlier than mama. "What did I do wrong to be punished like this? Did this happen to me because I hate Mr. Fred?" I turned and noticed that Mama had left the room.

I picked up a calendar and put a big X on the day I saw the first drop of blood. By the time September came I knew that the painful pimple on my chin meant it was almost time for my monthly to start. It was so annoying to keep up with that calendar, remember to ask Mama to buy a box of Kotex, and try to hide that ugly pimple on my chin. No amount of squeezing would make that big painful pimple go away.

During my first week back at Wardlow Elementary, my sixth grade teacher, Mrs. Houston, sent all the boys out of the classroom and then showed the girls a film about menstruation. I struggled to pronounce the word "menstruation" as I secretly tried to memorize the spelling and figure out why the word contained the silent letter u.

"Raise your hand if you've got your period?" Mrs. Houston asked.

A few girls raised their hands and quickly put them down. I didn't have a clue what the teacher was talking about. Mama had told me about a "monthly" – not a "period" so I didn't connect the two words right away. When I realized Mrs. Houston was referring to my monthly, I still didn't raise my hand because I was too ashamed to let anybody know that I was going to have a baby. Secretly, I admired the girls who were brave enough to raise their hands.

We watched the film on menstruation in complete silence until we saw millions of sperm, ejected from a penis, swimming rapidly toward an egg. The male's sperm were racing to be the first one to reach the female's egg. When one sperm reached the egg all the rest admitted defeat and gave up. Then a transformation in the egg began. Everybody gasped when the egg quickly changed into a baby. I guess we all thought the graphic presentation was revealing too much information.

The film taught me that the menstrual cycle or menstrual period occurred every 28 days, and that it was simply the time when blood and tissue are discharged from the vagina if you're NOT going to have a baby. By watching the film I learned that I had two openings in my private area – one for bleeding and another one for urinating. I was fascinated by what I learned about my own body.

After viewing the film, some girls proudly told the class about the first time they got their period.

Quiet Minnie said, "I tear up old clothes every month to get ready for my red-haired grandma to come pay me a visit."

"Yep, me too!" her cousin Catherine said. "One time I couldn't find the scissors so I had to cut the edges of an old sheet with a razor blade and rip the pieces apart."

"My mama had me cut up an old sheet into squares and keep them folded in the dresser drawer until I got my period," said Roxanne, the oldest girl in the class. This was her third year in sixth grade.

I was surprised to hear that she had prepared for her period before it even happened.

"Tell us how you dispose of the rags?" Mrs. Houston asked.

At that moment I realized that the teacher was asking her students to teach their classmates what they already knew.

My friend Nora, who never mentioned she'd gotten her period, blurted out, "I throw them in a hole in the backyard and burn them every month."

"I drop them in the outdoor toilet with all that other sh.., I mean, crap," Loretta said.

The whole class laughed at the humorous way she said it.

I listened carefully to everything my classmates shared. Nobody mentioned anything about having a baby. That day I learned that all girls get their period. Thank goodness! I thought. I sighed with relief in knowing I wasn't going to have a baby after all. I wondered why Mama didn't just say, *"Stay away from boys."* Now I know what she meant when she told my big sister Beverly, "Keep them panties up and your dress down."

I never told anyone that I feared I was going to have a baby. That would have made both my Mama and me look stupid. I was also thankful for the box of Kotex Mama kept in the bottom of the chifforobe. I actually felt a bit better off financially than some of my classmates because I wore soft Kotex sanitary napkins instead of old rags every month.

Who would have thought that I could be better off than someone else? I asked myself. The class discussion made me feel much better about myself. I could have jumped for joy as I shouted in my mind, "I'm a normal girl!"

I was happy all day. That is, until my excitement fizzled while I sat in social studies class that afternoon.

"Hawaii is the forty-ninth state in the United States," Mrs. Houston said.

My hand automatically flew up and I blurted, "My fifth grade teacher told us Alaska is the forty-ninth state."

"I know your fifth grade teacher and she doesn't know everything," Mrs. Houston retorted.

My classmates laughed at me for daring to correct the teacher. I wished I were a turtle so I could crawl back into my shell and hide. I kept my mouth shut for the rest of the day. I left school feeling bad about mentioning my beloved fifth grade teacher, Mrs. Collins, even though I hadn't called her name.

The following day in social studies class after everyone was seated, Mrs. Houston stood up, paused, and looked straight at us. She started talking slowly as she walked over and stood right in front of my desk in the front row.

"Yesterday, I made a mistake for which I am very sorry," she said. She looked straight at me. "Davida, your fifth grade teacher was correct. Alaska is the forty-ninth state and Hawaii is the fiftieth state." She looked around the classroom and said, "I want all of you to feel like you can correct me, like Davida did, if I say something wrong."

It was so quiet in that classroom that you could have heard a safety pin fall on the floor. I stared at my teacher in disbelief. She actually admitted she was wrong. "Wow!"

At the end of class Mrs. Houston called me up to her desk. "Davida, I want you to strive to rise above your circumstances."

I thought she was referring to my family being poor and I trembled.

"You have tremendous potential for success," she said. "You listen and retai what you learn."

I nodded, "Thank you, Ma'am." I turned to leave with a triumphant grin on my face.

Not only did I leave class that day with renewed confidence in my fifth grade teacher, but I felt like it was okay to speak up whenever I believed I was right. Mrs. Houston had given us the challenge to learn our lessons well enough so that nobody could make us believe something that wasn't true. I realized that knowledge gives a person confidence to speak up and command attention.

"I'm going to learn all I can so I will know what I'm talking about when I speak," I said. I was also proud of Mrs. Houston for admitting that she was wrong in front of the whole class. I could tell that it was a very difficult thing for her to say. My teacher's got guts! I thought.

Another teacher thinks I'll be successful! I told myself. I wonder if all my teachers get together and talk about their students. They all say the same thing.

I felt ready for anything life would bring my way. I just had no idea about the surprises that would challenge my faith and break my heart in the very near future.

CHAPTER 13

I RAN DOWN THE HILL and peeked through the front screen door looking for Grandpa Cox. He was usually outside working in the yard before sunrise on his day off, but not today.

"That's funny," I said when I saw my grandparents sitting beside each other on the couch. I pulled open the screen door and tiptoed inside to take a closer look.

I tried in vain to recall a time when I'd ever seen Grandpa Cox just sitting around doing nothing. My presence startled Grandma. She lifted her head off her husband's upper arm and blinked her puffy eyes.

"What's going on in here?" I asked.

"Willie called this morning to say my sister passed away in her sleep last night," Grandma Cox said. And they had to rush Lucille to the hospital when they told her the news. Lucille is low sick now and she might not make it either."

"Oh Grandma!" I sobbed, "I'm so sorry."

I sat down beside her and leaned my head against her arm. My crying seemed to make Grandma cry even harder. I couldn't help thinking they were both fine before they moved to Washington with Willie in June. It's only September and now Aunt Lula Belle is dead and Aunt Lucille is "low sick." I wonder if Willie took good care of them like he was supposed to. I sat quietly beside Grandma Cox feeling guilty for thinking my aunts would still be alive if they had stayed in Frazier Terrace.

After a long time Grandma stood up and said, "I'm gonna fix breakfast.

"All Right if you feel up to it," Grandpa told her. I'll go out in da barn if you don't need me right now."

He stood, clasped his hands, and stretched his long arms above his head. The distinct sound of cracking knuckles made me think he had been sitting in the same position for a long time. I followed Grandma into the kitchen as Grandpa headed for the front door. When the phone rang, he stopped in his tracks and listened. Four long rings meant the call was for them on their eight-party-line.

Grandpa picked up the receiver and grumbled, "Who dis?" He stood listening with his back turned to us as we stared at him from the kitchen.

He hung up the phone and then turned and limped toward us. "Justine," Grandpa said as he stood in the doorway shaking his head. "Dat was Willie again. I got mo bad news. Lucille didn't make it."

"Oh Jesus!" Grandma Cox cried, "Give me strength to carry on!"

Grandma gripped the edge of the kitchen table, I guess to break her fall if she fainted. I stood there wondering what I could do to help her. Grandpa limped toward her and she waved her hand to shoo him away.

"You go on out and handle yo business," she told him. "I'll be all right."

"You sho?" Grandpa sounded scared for her.

"The good Lord giveth and the good Lord taketh away," Grandma answered. "Blessed be the name of the Lord. I kinda 'pected them two to go 'round the same time since they been together so long."

Grandpa's piercing eyes followed every move she made. She turned on the oven and the biggest eye on their electric stove. After a few minutes, he turned and hobbled away.

"Are you going to the funeral in Washington, D.C.?" I asked Grandma.

"No! I ain't never been out of Sous Ca'lina in my life," she said. "And I'm thinking my sister died 'cause she was homesick."

"Ummmmm," I said.

Grandma got a can of Eatwell Sardines out of the cupboard and made some salmon croquettes. She made dough in her favorite dark green mixing bowl and spread it out on wax paper with a rolling pin. She cut out each biscuit and made neat rows of four on the baking sheet. After she slid the pan in the hot oven, she cleaned up her mess. In a few minutes, the smell of fried fish, fresh baked biscuits and perking coffee filled the air.

Cooking must be a good way to forget about your problems, I thought.

"Go fetch your grandpa," she said. "Tell him breakfast ready."

I ran outside hollering, "Breakfast is ready, Grandpa."

He stuck his pitchfork in the ground beside the barn and came right away. I walked back inside with him because I wasn't about to miss out on all that good food. Eating must be another good way to forget about your problems, I thought, while gobbling down hot biscuits with apple butter, salmon croquettes and grits.

None of our relatives from South Carolina went up north to the double funeral. I knew I couldn't go even if I wanted to. I couldn't help wondering if my aunts would still be alive if they hadn't moved to Washington. Since I'll never know, I'll just keep both of them alive by remembering the good times we shared.

The following Monday Grandpa brought home something special for his grandchildren that the white people he worked for had thrown away.

"One man's trash is another man's treasure," Grandpa bragged while giving me the assignment of turning his trash into toy treasures.

That evening I helped Harry remove two bald tires with round patches of yellow thread beneath the rubber from the back of Grandpa's pickup. We removed the black inflated inner tubes and put them on the ground so my little sisters could have fun bouncing on them. They made great trampolines.

"Thought I'd use them tires to make a big fire 'neath the black wash pot outdoors so Justine kin have plenty boiling water for her white clothes," Grandpa said. "What ya'll gonna do wid 'em?"

Harry and I stared at each other. Instantly, I thought of a better use for the tires.

"Let's you and I hold a tire like this and let Gladys or Barbara Jean climb inside. Then we can race the tires.

"That's a good idea, Sis," Harry said.

The girls giggled as they ran from the trampoline and climbed inside each of our tires.

"On your mark, get ready, get set, go!" Vera shouted as soon as the girls settled down inside the tires.

Both Harry and I gave our tire a strong push at the same time, then chased it as the tire rolled down the hill toward Grandpa's house. When the rubber tire bounced off the side of the house, the girls fell out on the ground. When Gladys and Barbara Jean got up they were dizzy. We laughed like crazy to see them walk around in circles like a chicken with its head cut off.

After the girls had their fun, Harry and I had a race.

"On your mark! Get ready! Get set! Go!" Vera shouted again.

We were off and running. We pushed the empty tires along a straight path to be the first one to cross the finish line which was a stick lying across the road. My palms were black and dirty when my tire crossed the finish line just a second ahead of Harry's tire.

"I beat you! I beat you! " I shouted as I jumped up and down for joy.

Grandpa stood in the front yard clapping. I'm sure that he brought junk home because he enjoyed watching us make toys out of it.

As soon as Grandpa said, "Show me what ya kin make wid dis," my creative juices began flowing. I started expecting him to bring home something his boss had thrown away every day. When I saw what he brought, the first thing I did was to think about what to do with it. When I thought of something I shared my ideas with Harry. Sometimes Vera and April made suggestions too. In fact, Vera was the first one to use the 78 records as flying saucers. It was good to know that Grandpa always thought of us and that we could put our heads together and come up with some great ideas.

"Grandpa's boss has a lot of stuff to throw away," I murmured as I tried to figure out what to do with a wooden crate that once contained heads of lettuce. Then I got an idea.

I turned the crate vertically and cut a hole in the top so we could have a puppet show. My little sisters took turns crawling into the plywood crate as the puppeteer. I put a white sock on Barbara Jean's hand and opened the door so she could stand inside the crate and hold a white puppet through the hole. I talked for the puppet. After we rehearsed for a puppet show, we set up the crate in the front yard to entertain our grandparents. I had fun using my voice to tell different stories.

Barbara Jean was the puppeteer when I was telling the story of Little Miss Muffet.

"Along came a spider and sat down beside her!" I said that part like it was scary.

Then I tapped the top of the crate and Barbara Jean got frightened. My puppet disappeared when she screamed and ran out of that crate.

"Ha, ha, ha!" Grandpa roared with laughter. "Dat child think dat spider's real!" he said as he got up and limped inside his house following Grandma.

"This is too much fun!" I shouted.

"Yea," Harry confessed. "But it still don't beat the flying saucers you brought us."

I beamed from ear to ear when I heard how much Harry liked the 78 records I brought home from Aunt Lucille and Aunt Lula Belle's house. "I'm glad you liked them," I said. "Our aunties are probably up in heaven smiling to hear you say that. Too bad they couldn't see us playing with them."

Thoughts of both my aunts dying made me not want to play anymore. I went inside the house and saw Grandpa sitting at the table.

Watching Grandpa in the kitchen was more fun than playing with any of his trash treasures. He liked his plate piled high with food and he slurped it up in a hurry.

"A big man need a big meal," he said after a big burp.

"Never eat or drink behind other people 'cause you get their germs," Mama had told us. I knew she didn't learn that from her papa 'cause he was quick to shove his spoon in our mouths.

"You chillen wanna taste dis?" he asked as we stood watching him like young chicks gathered around a mother hen. We were eager to get just a tidbit of whatever he was eating.

"Yes, Sir!" we all said at the same time. That is, unless he had some chunky hominy grits or Cream of Wheat. Then I shook my head and said, "No thanks. Grits I like. But that runny hominy is food for the birds."

I looked forward to Friday evening when Grandpa Cox whipped up a pitcher of homemade eggnog. He liked to celebrate the end of the workweek.

"Now here's how you make eggnog," Grandpa said. "First crack two or three fresh raw eggs like dis."

He squeezed each egg a special way in one hand instead of tapping the shell with a fork like Grandma and Mama did. I was amazed that he could crack the eggshell without spilling one drop. He took my hand and tried to show me how he did it, but I didn't get it, so I just watched him after that.

Grandpa dumped the eggs into a thick glass pitcher that looked like a tall measuring cup and added a few spoons of sugar, nutmeg, vanilla flavor, and milk. Grandpa secretly added his special ingredient that he kept hidden in the kitchen cupboard behind the canned goods. He screwed off the cap of a half-pint glass bottle of brown whiskey. He took a sip from the bottle, licked his lips and smacked them real loud, and made an ugly face like the stuff was killing him. Then he wiped his mouth with the back of his hand.

Next he poured a dab of whiskey into the eggnog and screwed the bottle cap back on tight, then hid the bottle back in the cupboard. He stirred the drink briskly with a fork that made a clanging noise against the sides of the glass pitcher. Finally, he took a sip, licked his lips again and leaned back in his chair.

"Ahhhh," he said.

After the eggnog passed his taste test, he filled his favorite metal eggnog cup and held it to every child's lips so we could taste his drink.

"Here, take a sip," Grandpa said. Anybody who didn't know him would think he was mean because his gruff voice sounded so harsh. "It got eggs in it. Eggs good for ya! They make ya strong like milk."

Sometimes his eggnog concoction tasted better than other times. I'm pretty sure that more or less sugar or whiskey made the difference.

I loved my grandpa. He treated me like I was his little girl. Spending time with him helped me not to miss my daddy too much. No wonder Mama always talked about her papa. He must have been a good daddy to her when she was little. I tried to imagine how life would be if we still lived with Daddy. I missed him so much.

The moment I thought about Daddy, I told myself, "He's been gone for a long time. It's hard to believe that Daddy is never coming back home. Grandpa is my new daddy." I struggled with replacing Daddy with another man. But Grandpa deserved that special place in my heart because he spent time with us. That meant more than any gift he could ever give us.

On the other hand, I had mixed feelings about the way I felt about Grandma Cox. Most of the time she wore an apron while she worked in the garden, washed clothes, cooked meals, canned fruits and vegetables, and cleaned her house. But when it was time for her husband to come home she freshened up and served him. I knew I didn't love her as much as I loved Grandpa because she had very little to say when I was around. I knew she dressed up in long dresses and wide-brimmed straw hats when she went shopping or over to Uncle Clyde's house. But I didn't feel like I knew her very well. The one thing I did know was that whenever she left home, she always came back in time to have Grandpa's hot dinner ready when he came in from work.

Grandma sat and silently watched Grandpa talk to us and feed us. The only thing she said clearly was, "It's time for you children to go home." I don't think she liked us hanging around her too long because one day I heard her telling somebody on the other end of the telephone, "Sometimes these children get on my nerves."

I tried to stay out of her way. Even Mama didn't come next door to visit her parents very often and I don't remember ever seeing my grandma inside our house. Maybe she doesn't like children anymore now that all of hers are grown, I thought. She was much nicer to us when we came to visit her once in a while.

One day while I was sitting in the living room at Uncle Clyde's house, I happened to notice a large family portrait on the mantle. His two daughters had on the prettiest dresses I had ever seen in my life. My only brother, Harry, didn't even have a suit, but Uncle Clyde's two sons had on dress suits with shirts and neckties. At that moment, I realized that my family had never taken a picture together. We never dressed up for a photograph other than our school pictures.

"Where did you get those pretty dresses?" I asked, not really expecting an answer.

"Grandma gave them to us," my tall and skinny cousin Olivia, proudly replied with a huge grin. I think she could tell I was jealous.

"Which grandma?" I asked, while thinking, *Aunt Judy's mother sure has good taste.* I knew she wasn't talking about Grandma Cox because she never gave us anything. And we live right next door to her.

"Grandma Cox gave the boys suits, shirts and neck ties. She gave the girls dresses with matching socks and patent leather shoes."

"Dang!" My feelings were hurt but I tried not to show it. I was shocked to learn that my grandma shopped for Uncle Clyde's children's clothes and gave them gifts. I can't wait to tell Mama about this! Although I smiled during the rest of my visit, I was burning with anger. That news made me sick to my stomach.

The moment I walked through our backdoor and saw Mama at the kitchen stove I blurted, "Mama, you won't believe what I just saw! Uncle Clyde has a family portrait and his girls are wearing beautiful dresses and the boys have on new suits that Grandma Cox gave them! How is it that we live right next door to her and she never gave us any clothes?"

Mama turned and looked at me as if my news was not at all surprising to her.

"My mama gave me a bolt of red and white candy-striped cloth one time," Mama said. I made all the girls a dress and Harry a shirt from the same material...."

My mind flashed back to the red and white candy-striped dress that got burned up when our house burned down in Marshall Village.

"My mama never liked me because my papa loves me," Mama said. She choked on her words like it hurt her to talk about it.

"What?" I asked.

"She always treated my five brothers special but only papa treated me special. I guess she's jealous of anybody that papa loves—like my half-sister's mother."

"Do you know your half-sister?" I asked. "I've never seen her before."

Mama chuckled, "Oh, I almost forgot I was frying bacon." She turned back to the wood burning stove and continued talking while flipping each slice of the delicious smelling bacon as hot grease popped from a heavy black skillet. Mama backed away from the stove every time the popping sound got real loud.

"Child, I'm telling you, my papa was no different from your daddy," she said. "All men like to chase women."

I didn't appreciate Mama saying bad things about my Grandpa or my daddy. I thought she was wrong about her mother's behavior toward her too so I spoke up.

"Maybe Grandma's angry with you because you left Gladys at her house for awhile when she was a baby. Maybe the crying baby got on her nerves. Or maybe she's angry because you have too many children for her to buy clothes for and she doesn't have that much money."

"I just told you my mama don't like me because my papa loves me," Mama snapped at me like she was going to bite my head off. "She didn't like me when I was growing up."

"My goodness! I can't understand how a mother would not like her own child." I turned and walked away with tears in my eyes, trying to picture in my mind how Grandma Cox could mistreat her only daughter. Oh, but look how different she treats her own grandchildren, I thought. Don't parents know it hurts children to feel slighted? Even though my mama was a pretty girl, she might not have felt good about herself because her own mama hated her.

I walked outside and stared up at the blue sky decorated with a few white cotton balls. I'll bet Mama had a lot of babies so she could have a lot of people to love her, I thought. Then I felt sorry for my mama.

Nobody else knew that Grandma had given special gifts to Uncle Clyde's children and I knew better than to talk about it anymore. "I guess it was meant for me to find out," I mumbled. "Lord, why do I have to be the first one to discover bad things?"

CHAPTER 14

EARLY ON FEBRUARY 4, 1960, when I was twelve
years old, I went outside to catch the school bus. I noticed
that Grandpa's truck was still parked in the driveway. It
was Grandpa's seventieth birthday so I ran down the hill
to wish him a quick happy birthday before going to the
bus stop.

"Maybe he took the day off work to celebrate," I said,
as I stepped into the living room.

I froze when I saw Grandpa Cox limping out of his
bedroom wearing only his long johns. His gaze was on
the front door and his mind seemed to be somewhere
else. His eyes were wide open but he didn't even glance
at me even though I was standing only a foot away as he
hobbled past me without his cane. I was standing in plain
sight holding books in my arms.

"Happy birthday, Grandpa!" I whispered to avoid
startling him.

He said nothing. He didn't even look in my direction.
I thought it was quite odd that Grandpa hadn't slipped
on a pair of trousers over his long johns. I glanced at the
open bedroom door and saw his trousers still hanging on
the footboard of his bed.

Grandpa Cox pushed the screen door open but stopped
at the threshold. He stuck his head out and looked around
outside as though he was looking for someone who had
knocked. Seeing no one, he turned and limped back past
me to the bedroom and went back to bed.

I heard Grandma running water in the kitchen moments before I heard the school bus shift gears outside.
Just then, the bus horn blew and I ran outside closing the
front door behind me. I dashed up the hill to catch the
school bus that had already pulled away from our stop.

The driver saw me running as fast as I could and made a jerky stop that made the students holler.

"Thank you for waiting for me," I panted. I rushed to my seat as the bus driver scraped the gears and pulled off.

"Whew!" I panted, dropping down on the cold leather seat. All the way to school I tried to answer questions about my morning visit to Grandpa. Why didn't Grandpa see me? Was he sick? Was he blind? Was I invisible? I couldn't figure it out.

* * *

After school I rushed inside our house when I saw Grandpa's pickup still parked in the driveway. I was thinking, *I'll put my books away, change clothes and then go give Grandpa the proper happy birthday I didn't give him this morning.*

"Why is Grandpa's truck still here" I asked Mama.

"Papa died this morning," Mama said sadly from her seat behind the sewing machine. "And he wasn't even sick."

My heart skipped a beat and then dropped into my stomach. "How?" I cried. "He walked to the door and looked out this morning like he'd heard somebody knock. He was fine then."

Mama stopped stitching and looked up at me. "Papa was late leaving for work, so I went down to check on him right after your school bus pulled off," Mama said. "Papa was already dead in his bed. My mama was in the kitchen cooking breakfast. She thought he took the day off work 'cause it's his birthday."

I realized that I had been the last person to see Grandpa alive. "Grandpa didn't see me this morning even though I could have reached out and touched him," I stammered. "He must have heard Jesus knocking on the front door when he looked outside. Grandma was in the kitchen cooking but she didn't seem to hear anybody knock. She didn't even hear me come inside. I wonder why she didn't hear what Grandpa heard."

"Cause the second coming of Jesus is when he comes back for you." Mama said. "Papa answered when he heard his name called this morning."

"Where's Grandpa now?" I asked.

"His body is at Foster's Funeral Home. The undertaker picked it up this morning. My papa's gone home to be with Jesus."

"How's Grandma taking it?" I asked.

"W-e-l-l," Mama said slowly, "I don't know if Mama's gonna make it without Papa. She loved that man."

* * *

That afternoon, I stood in the living room looking down at Mama seated behind her Singer sewing machine. The smell of freshly baked cornbread drifting from the kitchen made me want to puke. Food lost its meaning without my grandpa. I stared at Mama waiting for her to tell me more. She just put her foot on the sewing machine pedal and it whirred as she pulled the fabric beneath the needle.

I stared at Mama, thinking about how much Grandpa meant to us and how life was about to change for Grandma too. Grandma had just lost her husband of fifty years. The man who had made Grandma, Mama and me feel so special was gone forever.

"All the men in our family keep leaving us!" I yelled angrily as I slid into a corner of the sofa and broke down and cried. I cried for a long time. I couldn't stop. My little sisters leaned against me and cried too.

I heard Mama sniffing. She got up and went into the kitchen, then came back a few minutes later and put a plate of pinto beans and rice, bacon and cornbread in my lap.

"Food will make you feel stronger," she said.

"I don't want food!" I shouted, "I want my grandpa!"

Mama took the plate out of my lap and put it back in the kitchen. She sat down and started sewing again while I kept on crying.

I didn't eat anything that evening. I wasn't hungry at all. I didn't go next door either because I couldn't bear the thought of being in that house without Grandpa being there.

Mama took some food next door to her mother. I could tell that it was real hard for Mama to wait on her mother after the way Grandma had always treated her.

It was three weeks after Grandpa's funeral before I was strong enough to go next door to visit Grandma Cox. By then I think my grandma had lost her mind. She missed Grandpa Cox a whole lot more than I could even imagine. She couldn't cope with being alone in her house so she stayed outside all day long – just walking aimlessly around in the yard. She didn't cook and she didn't eat the food Mama sent to her. With all her sons out of town and Uncle Clyde at work, Mama was the one who had to help Grandma.

That's funny. Grandma loves her sons and hates her daughter, but it's the daughter who's taking care of her. In this life you never know how things will turn out.

Every day, Grandma's hands and clothes got filthier and filthier. She roamed around outdoors like an animal. Mama would go next door to clean her up, but Grandma pushed over the white hand basin, jerked her head away from Mama, and snatched the wet wash rag so her face couldn't get washed. My grandma was little, but she was strong. Mama tried to feed her with a spoon but Grandma sealed her lips shut tight and pushed the spoon away. Mama waited until she opened her mouth and then shoved food in it, but Grandma would spit the food out as soon as she tasted it.

Mama cooked every day but she got tired of fighting with Grandma, who got meaner and meaner. Grandma didn't do what was best for her and nobody could tell her anything. When I took Grandma her plate, I saw yesterday's food still on the table, untouched, except for ants crawling all over it.

As weeks turned into months, Grandma started leaning her head forward when she walked and her back curved like a turtle's shell. She looked like she might fall with every step. Soon, she was crawling around outdoors in her long dresses with an apron tied around her waist. When I went to lift her up, her hands and feet were hard and rough like the shell of a turtle. She didn't clean her house, bathe, brush her teeth, comb her hair, or even change her clothes anymore.

"Grandma, may I bathe you," I whispered one afternoon after I picked her up off the ground to guide her into the house.

She snapped, "Git outta here! Go home!" My grandma seemed to have absolutely no reason to go on living.

Harry and my little sisters were with me that day, sitting on Grandma's metal swing on the front porch. They held their nose while I helped Grandma walk through the front door. Both Barbara Jean and Carrie told her bluntly, "Grandma, you stink!"

Grandma kept on walking without saying a word.

Mama followed us inside. "She won't let me bathe her," Mama said.

"Why don't you put Grandma in a hospital?" I asked.

Grandma plopped down on the side of her filthy bedspread.

"She can't go in the hospital 'cause she's not sick. She's just mourning the passing of her husband."

"How long before she stops mourning?" Harry asked. He surprised me because I usually asked all the questions.

"Nobody knows," Mama mumbled. "We'll just have to wait and see. People have to live until they die. I know she won't eat her food and a person's got to eat to stay alive."

"Maybe Uncle Clyde can make her take a bath and eat," I said.

"I told him she fights me when I try to help her," Mama said. "My brother's too busy to come see about his mama. He told me to do whatever I need to do."

Nobody seemed to know what to do about Grandma's condition. So, they left her alone. She continued to live in her house all alone and she slept in her dirty clothes every night. It stank too bad in that house for anybody else to stay with her.

The next afternoon, I was embarrassed to see my grandma lying on the ground when the school bus stopped in front of my house. She lay curled up in the yard like a big, dirty ball of old clothes. All the students on the school bus stared at her but I was glad nobody laughed, at least not while I was on the bus.

Grandma started crawling on the ground like a dog sniffing for a buried bone. I was convinced that she was searching for Grandpa's buried body. It was hard to believe that Grandma, who had always been a strong, clean woman, became completely helpless as soon as her husband died.

I pretended to read a book as the school bus came to my stop because I was certain that everybody knew the lady lying outside on the ground was my grandma. I made a silent plea, "God, please don't let anybody say a bad word about her!" Nobody said a bad word. They probably felt sorry for her like I did when they saw her sniffing the dirt. Only a fool would not realize that something was seriously wrong with her, I thought. The same thing could happen to their grandmother too.

The next afternoon as the school bus rounded a bend near my stop, I saw Grandma lying on the edge of the road. I gasped in horror as the bus swerved to avoid hitting her. All the other times she had stayed in the yard. But this time she lay on the edge of the road. It seemed like she was trying to commit suicide. Students on my side of the bus saw her too and screamed, especially when the bus swerved. Instantly, I started thinking of ways to get her safely back in the yard. When the bus stopped, I hopped off and dropped my books beside the road and ran over to help lift Grandma's head out of danger.

"It's me, Grandma, it's Davida."

She opened her eyes and seemed to be looking at someone far away, although I was the only one standing in front of her. I strained to help her sit up.

"I'm going to take you back in the yard where it's safe," I whispered. "You could get run over by a car out here." I saw in her eyes a frightened little child as her trembling hand grasped my arm and clung to it.

"I'm here, Grandma, I'm here," I said softly. By that time Harry, Vera, April and Gladys had gathered around to help me.

"I'm going to spread my legs." I showed them how as I straddled Grandma's body. "Don't let me fall if I stumble back when I pull Grandma's arms. I need two of you to hold my right leg and two to hold my left leg."

My sisters and Harry thought I had made up another game for us to play. I pulled Grandma's arms real hard and walked backwards. The others walked with me as I counted one, two, three! It was just like when I pulled Aunt Lucille to her seat. It had been easier with Aunt Lucille because she was sitting in a chair or on the sofa.

As I strained to pull her up, Harry left Vera at my leg and ran behind Grandma's back and pushed like he did when he pushed the wagon loaded with logs. He helped to hoist Grandma to her feet. I was so glad he thought to do that even though he made some ugly faces.

"Go get my books," I told Vera and April after we were safely in the yard.

Vera and April ran up the hill and picked them up. Then they followed at a distance as Harry and I escorted Grandma toward the house. I had my arm around Grandma on the left and Harry walked close to her right side without touching her. Gladys ran ahead of us to open the screen door as we entered the house. Mama had moved Grandma's bed into the living room so I only needed to take a few steps before I eased her down on her bed.

While we were outside, the stench was so strong that I held my breath. Inside, I found myself all alone with Grandma. The others abandoned me the moment the strong odor of bottled up pee and poop blasted us at the door. I'd learned in science class that the nose adapts to stink odors in about thirty seconds. That was helpful because I knew right away that Grandma had done number one and number two in her pants. For me to clean her up, my nose had to adapt to the odor.

I untied Grandma's apron and opened the buttons in the front of her dress. I laid her on her back so I could remove her wet panties. Fresh poop had run down her legs. I heated a pot of water while searching for some clean clothes. It was no fun cleaning up that stuff but I figured somebody had to do it. I thought, *If I can change Mama's babies, then I can change her mama too.*

Dang! I sure wish they made diapers big enough for grownups! I thought.

Grandma didn't fight me when I wiped the layers of fresh, crusty brown mess from between her legs. After I washed her up and put clean clothes on her, I changed her sheets and bedspread and took the filthy clothes outside and set them on fire.

Vera came outside after I started the fire in the yard. "How could you stay in Grandma's house so long," she asked.

"Cause I kept asking God to let me see a stink baby, and not my grandma," I answered. "That's how I did it."

"How'd it go with mama?" Mama yelled from the kitchen doorway.

"I picked Grandma up out of the street today and she didn't try to fight me," I said cheerfully, thinking my Grandma was coming back to her normal self.

"Good for you!" Mama said sarcastically. I think she thought I was bragging about being able to get her mother to cooperate with me when she couldn't do it.

* * *

Mama continued to prepare meals and send food to her mother every day by one of us children, but Grandma steadily lost weight and became more and more feeble.

She wouldn't eat even when we cut her food in tiny pieces and tried to feed her. She just kept her lips shut and turned her head. At first Grandma used to fuss, but she even stopped talking.

The day Grandma quit talking I lay awake late that night thinking about how people act when somebody dies. I guess every person grieves differently when a loved one dies. Mama kept on going because she had to take care of business, her mother, and her family. Sewing was her way of keeping herself together. On the other hand, Grandma's reason for living had died and was buried. She seemed to be trying to kill herself.

Uncle Clyde never came to visit at all after Grandpa died. He told Mama, "I don't want to see my ma in bad shape. I know how much she loved papa."

"I don't understand him," I mumbled. "Would he rather see her dead? He must have forgotten that somebody has to take care of people in bad shape. Only God knows where Mama's other brothers are. Shouldn't family help each other when somebody dies? What about us? I miss Grandpa too, but nobody cares about how we feel because we're just children."

Teardrops trickled across my ear and wet my pillowcase. I rolled onto my side, away from the wet spot, and cried.

"I need to get away from here," I sobbed. "But where can I go?" I looked up at the ceiling where moonlight played as it bounced over the tree branches swaying in the night breeze. Moonlight also sneaked through a tiny hole in our tin roof, the one we put a bucket beneath every time it rained. I began thinking about my life before we moved to the country.

CHAPTER 15

I SQUIRMED ON MY SOFA BED staring at the darkness, thinking about my life before it turned sour. Daddy claimed that I was his special gift because the midwife didn't show up until after he had already brought me into the world. When the midwife arrived, she told my parents they should name me Davida, after my daddy, David. Mama said, "Davida Kincaid had a nice ring to it that tickled her ears." So that's how I got the name, Davida.

"You're the only Davida I know," Mama said.

That news made me feel special because I was Mama's eighth child. It was an honor to be the only child in my family named after my daddy. At least, that was the case until my little brother, Harry, was born about two years later. My parents named him David Harry Kincaid, Jr. but everybody called him Harry because he had a lot of hair all over his body when he was born.

Even after all the babies in our house, Mama still attracted men's attention with her tiny waist and big behind. Women still called my daddy handsome. Getting married doesn't stop a person from being attractive to other people.

One day, we were riding in Uncle Clyde's pickup on our way to the country where Grandpa and Grandma Cox lived, when I overheard Mama talking about Daddy.

"My husband planned to leave his family just like his papa left his," Mama said. "Yeah, he was planning to run off to Washington with a girl down in Orangeburg when he got his paycheck on Friday. So I packed my suitcase while he was at his meatpacking job and caught the Greyhound to Columbia. I brought my two youngest children with me. I left all the other children for David and his girlfriend to decide what to do with them. I beat my husband at his own game!" Mama declared.

Mama was right because Daddy didn't run away to Washington, D.C.

Mama kept on talking. "David used his paycheck on Friday to get a neighbor to drive him and the older children up to Columbia. When he showed up at Mama and Papa's house asking me to come back home, I told him to prove that he wanted his family back again. Get a job in Columbia and find us our own house and then I'll believe you serious. You can stay up here but I ain't going back down to Orangeburg."

My daddy must have wanted his family back real bad because he found a job as a garbage man with the City of Columbia the day after he arrived. Mama and all her children stayed at my grandparents' house while Daddy went to stay with Mama's brother Clyde, who lived near a bus stop in Marshall Village. Daddy stayed there so he could ride the bus back and forth to work. Daddy's new boss man at the City Shed let him rent a duplex near Harden Street. On the next Saturday, Daddy collected his first pay in cash, and our whole family moved into a two-bedroom yellow board duplex with a big front yard. The house was in walking distance to Daddy's job in downtown Columbia.

Everybody in my family lived together in the duplex, except my sister Vickie. Nobody talked about the reason why Daddy had left her down in Orangeburg with Aunt Josephine.

Mama stayed at home while Daddy went to work picking up people's garbage every day except Sunday. It was easy to tell when Daddy was at home because he and Mama liked to argue. Daddy accused Mama of "flirting with another man," and Mama yelled back at him, "Two can play this game!"

I became as accustomed to hearing and seeing Mama and Daddy fight in our house as I was to the smell of Tide detergent in white cotton Birdseye diapers hanging on the clothesline, or the sight of glass bottles full of Carnation baby formula in the icebox. Yelling at each other began as soon as Daddy came home from work.

Mama and Daddy also fought whenever Daddy didn't like what Mama fixed for dinner, dinner wasn't ready yet and Daddy was hungry, Mama hadn't washed or ironed Daddy's uniform, Mama asked Daddy to fix a broken piece of furniture and he was too tired to do it, or crying babies hindered Daddy from getting his rest. Since there was no particular thing that triggered an argument, we watched and waited to see what would upset them. If we made it through dinner, there was always the possibility they would argue in their bedroom.

Mama and Daddy didn't stop with arguments. Sometimes they actually fought. Mama would hit Daddy with a brick or something. Lots of times I heard her yell at him from behind their closed bedroom door.

"You'd better not go to sleep or you won't wake up!" Mama shouted. "I'll throw boiling water in your face! We'll see what woman wants you then!"

"You better be glad you a woman," Daddy liked to say. "Or I'd knock you out."

A little while later, I could hear Daddy's snores followed by Mama's, like a musical call and response. Their snores might have brought relief to them but they didn't help me go back to sleep. I just lay on my back wide-awake staring at the ceiling where I saw figures dancing in the dark. I guess everyone in our room was asleep but me. I wondered how they could sleep through all that noise.

It frightened me when Mama and Daddy fought. The fights didn't seem to bother Harry and my sisters so much. But I was afraid Daddy would get hurt. He seemed to underestimate Mama's strength. I know that once or twice Mama popped my fanny with her bare hand and it was stinging for a long time. Mama always let Daddy give us a whupping when we did something wrong.

"You better be glad your daddy's the one whupping you," Mama said. "He's gentler than me."

***

I was scared to death that night when Daddy shoved Mama in the living room.

She stumbled backward with the baby in her arms. She looked up in his face, shook her head, and shouted, "I hate people thinking they can walk all over me just 'cause they're bigger than me." Mama dropped the baby in my lap as I sat watching them. She ran into the kitchen and ran right back clutching the block of wood that propped up the kitchen window sash.

I screamed as loud as I could, "Mama STOP!"

I covered my eyes with both hands because I couldn't bear to watch. I pictured Daddy's head rolling on the floor. There was silence. I peeked through my fingers when I heard the front door open. Mama didn't hit him, because Daddy walked out.

"Whew! That was close!" I said as my heart did a little dance to let me know it had been standing at attention and was now settling down.

Mama took the baby off my lap and said, "A man's stronger than a woman so you have to pick up something. You can't have a fair fight with your bare hands with somebody stronger than you."

* * *

After midnight, somebody climbed on our front porch while the house was quiet. I think everybody woke up when we heard a loud noise in the kitchen that sounded like something big had dropped on the floor. Mama's bed squeaked when she jumped up and rushed toward the kitchen. When she darted past our bedroom, we ran behind her. With the help of the moonlight shining through the window, we saw the outline of a stranger, a man lying down on the floor. Mama rushed right over and clobbered the man on the head with the straightening comb. The man screamed like a shot dog and then lay there like he was dead.

Mama leaned over him shaking the straightening comb. "You got no business coming in my house like that! You going to jail for breaking and entering!" Mama kicked his thigh.

Since we didn't have a telephone, Zenobia rushed over to the neighbor's duplex to call the police. We stood around watching and waiting, while Daddy kept on snoring in the bedroom. I noticed the kitchen window screen was missing. The man had pushed the sash all the way up when he crawled through the window.

Soon, Mama opened the door for a broad-hipped white police officer wearing a black uniform, knee-high black boots and a shiny silver badge on his shirt pocket.

The policeman shook the man. "Get up!" he shouted. He yanked the man's arms to help him stand up. Then he grabbed the groggy man's hands and put handcuffs on him. "Let's go!" he yelled as he pushed the short, young man who needed a shave out of the house ahead of him.

"You betta watch where you going from now on!" Mama scolded him as the policeman took the man away.

That straightening comb incident plus all of my parent's fights had made me a nervous wreck. I guess the drama terrified me more than the other children because I was younger, or maybe, because I was more timid. I really don't know why I was so scared. I only know that my big sister Lynette noticed how jumpy I was and that I had started biting my nails.

"It'll be all right," Lynette whispered. "Husbands and wives just get on each other's nerves for no special reason."

"I wish Mama and Daddy would stop fighting so much," I sobbed.

"I used to wish that too," she said, "but I'm used to it now."

I think my mama gave Daddy a reason for the fights. I never saw my daddy talking to another woman, but I knew very well that a man always came to talk to Mama in the backyard while Daddy was at work. Mama, and

Mr. Walter who lived somewhere in the row of houses behind our duplex, liked to put their faces close to each other. I could see both of them smiling as he leaned down and Mama stared up into his eyes. Mama and Mr. Walter seemed to enjoy talking to each other more than Mama and Daddy ever did. It was strange, but Mr. Walter suddenly appeared whenever Mama was pushing me on my favorite ride – a rubber tire swinging from a rope attached to a tree branch on our side of the duplex. Sometimes I didn't even realize it was Mr. Walter rather than Mama pushing my swing. I never saw him come or leave. I'd hear his voice and look back, and there he was.

Mr. Walter had a strange laugh like his insides were bubbling over. I never heard what Mama said, but he always found her words so funny. One time I heard him say in a deep voice, "Blossom, you're so funny! It's not what you say. It's the way you say it with your squeaky little voice. I could listen to you talk all day long." Then he roared with laughter. They talked a lot to each other but they never yelled like Mama and Daddy did.

I also thought it was strange that Mr. Walter always knew when we were outside. I wondered why he didn't have to go to work every day like my daddy. I usually played on the swing for a long time, and then Mama made me go inside to take my nap. Swinging always made me sleepy. When I woke up I could smell food. Mr. Walter was always gone when I went to the kitchen and found Mama in a cheerful mood. She was cooking or baking her delicious sweet biscuits, cornbread or homemade yeast rolls.

Mama liked to say, "The way to a man's heart is through his stomach." That's what she often told my big sisters when they helped her in the kitchen.

I noticed something else too. On the days when Mama was in a good mood, that's when she and Daddy fussed as soon as he came home from work. I think a neighborhood spy probably told Daddy that Mr. Walter had been spotted in our yard. If so, then I'm sure they fought because Mama denied it.

I'll never forget that day when Mama warned me, "Never mention Mr. Walter or I'll pop you good!" So, at five years old I learned how to keep secrets. I knew something didn't seem right with all the fighting in my house, but I didn't understand what was wrong.

* * *

I felt myself getting sleepy and turned on my back. My head sank into the middle of my feather pillow. Mama's warning about keeping a secret was the last thing I remembered.

CHAPTER 16

I MUST HAVE DOZED OFF for only a short time because when I woke up it was still dark in the living room. My pillow was wet behind my ears so I flipped it over. I guess I cried myself to sleep. I had been thinking about when I was five years old and Lynette walked up to me, stooped down and looked in my eyes.

"You got to be brave and strong like Mama," she said.

"All I want to do is have fun being a little girl," I told her.

"Well, I hope you get your wish," she said. Then she went inside the house and left me on the front porch.

"You wanna play hide and seek?" Harry said as soon as Lynette was out of sight.

"Yeah," I said. "You count to twenty first and I'll go hide."

While playing hide and seek with my little brother Harry I decided to follow Lynette's advice. I ran behind a neighbor's house where our friends lived in one duplex and another man, Mr. Knox, lived in the other side. I was looking for a good place to hide when Mr. Knox came walking in the yard.

"I forgot my key and I'm locked out," he said. "Can I put you through my window so you can unlock my door for me?"

I can do that quickly and still go and hide before Harry gets here, I thought.

"Yes, sir," I said.

Mr. Knox hoisted me to the windowsill like I was a chair. I crawled through the open window and jumped to the floor. I ran to the back porch, turned the doorknob and walked out in no time.

That was easy! I thought as I slapped my hands to signal completion of the job while walking down the three wooden steps.

Mr. Knox rushed up the steps past me, caught the door before it closed, and disappeared inside.

He didn't even say "thank you," I thought. "How impolite!"

I spotted a good hiding place behind a big silver garbage can at the corner of the duplex. Harry would never think to look for me there, I thought. I crouched behind the can until I got tired. After counting to one hundred and still no Harry, I gave up waiting and went back home where I found Harry sitting on the front porch.

As soon as Harry saw me, he stood up with a puzzled look on his face. "Davida, where'd you go?" He yelled.

I didn't answer. I laughed as I passed him with my head cocked in the air, proudly walking straight into our house. It felt good being a brave girl.

That night, as we were sitting at the kitchen table, Mama said, "Somebody stole some things out of Miss Eloise's house today and they didn't break in neither. The police took old Mr. Knox to jail. He's the man who lives on the other side of the duplex. Somebody saw him walk out Eloise back door with a lot of stuff in his arms."

I got scared. I thought Mr. Knox would tell the police that I had unlocked the door for him and they would come back and take me to jail too. My hands were shaking and I almost dropped my fork as I tried to sit still and look innocent.

All of a sudden there was a loud KNOCK, KNOCK, KNOCK at the front door. I dropped my fork in the plate and jumped up out of my chair. I just knew it had to be the police coming to get me.

"Davida, stop being such a fraidy cat!" Lynette said as she stared at me.

"Who is it?" Mama hollered as she rushed to the front door.

Oh, no! They're coming to get me! I panicked and ran behind our big white kitchen stove. While crouched there, I rehearsed what I would tell the police— *I didn't know it wasn't his side of the house. He tricked me.*

"It's me, Clyde!" my uncle yelled back.

Fear rolled away like water off a duck's back when I heard my uncle's voice. I breathed a big sigh of relief and slowly crawled from behind the stove as everybody stared at me, laughing. My appetite was gone, so I went into the living room and sat down beside my daddy who was talking to Uncle Clyde.

That night and for the next few nights, my secret caused me to have nightmares.

Lynette told me that I screamed out, "No! No! No!" in my sleep.

I know that I tossed and turned so much that I woke up and had trouble going back to sleep.

After I'd been screaming in my sleep for seven nights, I lay awake crying when Lynette came over in the dark and stood at the edge of my bunk bed beside me and patted my cheek.

"I won't let anything bother you," she whispered. "Just tell me what you see in your dreams. Talking about bad things is a good way to get it out of your mind so you can sleep peacefully at night." She stroked my cheek with her finger. I felt safe with her near me.

I'd better not tell her or she'll tell Daddy, I thought. But who else can I tell? She's the only one who seems to know I have bad dreams. "All right, I'll tell you if you think it will make my bad dreams go away," I whispered back in the dark.

"I know it will," Lynette whispered. "The truth will set you free. Now tell me."

"Every time I go to sleep I see myself alone in our room in my top bunk bed," I said. "There are lots of worms crawling all over the floor and I can't get out of the room without stepping on them 'cause they're crawling on the walls and the bedroom door too."

"What do they look like?" she asked.

"You know. Wiggly worms! Some are short and fat and fuzzy. Some are long and skinny like bait. Sometimes I see snakes crawling all in the house, even hanging from the ceiling and I'm afraid to get out of bed 'cause they're everywhere."

"Now don't you feel better?" she asked.

"Yeah," I said. Lynette was right. It felt so good to be able to talk to somebody.

"Now you ought to be able to go to sleep," she said. "Close your eyes and go to sleep. I'll stay right here with you for awhile."

I closed my eyes and I fell asleep. The next morning when I opened my eyes I saw Lynette sitting on the side of her bunk bed watching me.

"You slept like a baby," she said, smiling. "Is there anything else you want to tell me?" she asked.

I swallowed hard, so hard I could feel my throat get sore and dry. I stared into her big eyes. I sat up and hesitated. She got up and moved over closer to stand by my bunk. It felt good to have a big sister I could trust to listen to my secrets.

"I feel bad because I opened the door for Mr. Knox," I whispered.

Lynette listened like a good friend and she didn't fuss at me or call me stupid.

"Well, he's in jail now so you don't need to be afraid of him," she said. "Do you remember when you first started having the bad dreams?"

"It was the same night Mama said the police caught the man who stole stuff out of Miss Eloise's house without breaking in. Mr. Knox had put me through the open window to unlock the door for him."

"That dirty old man tricking an innocent child!" she said. "Were you scared he was coming to get you because you told on him?"

"No, I was scared the police was going to take me to jail too. That night I dreamt that worms were crawling all over me and I kept slapping my face to get them off."

"You poor baby," Lynette said and patted me on my head. "Don't worry about a thing."

"Please don't tell Daddy!" I sniffed. "I don't want a whupping with that strap."

"I won't tell a soul," she said stroking my cheek with her finger. "Your little secret is safe with me."

I didn't feel heavy anymore. I wasn't worried anymore. No wonder Mama said, "Confession is good for the soul."

I stopped having nightmares after our talk, but Lynette started teasing me and calling me a "fraidy cat" in front of everybody. I couldn't believe it.

"You better watch out, fraidy cat!" she jeered. "A worm is coming to get you!"

Every time she called me 'fraidy cat,' I felt ashamed that I had trusted Mr. Knox. I was sorry I'd trusted Lynette with my secret too. She only listened to me so she could get a good laugh. I made up my mind not to tell her anything else, so I quit talking to her.

* * *

One night, a week later, I was sitting next to Lynette at the kitchen table eating liver and onions. Suddenly Lynette put her arm around the back of my wooden chair and leaned over to take a close look at my hair. She seemed to be studying something in my hair.

"There's something in your hair!" she shrieked.

A hush fell around the table and everybody stopped eating and looked in my direction.

"What is it?" I said as I attempted to jump out of the chair but she pressed me down by my shoulders.

"Hold still!" she yelled. "Let me get it for you!"

I froze and waited anxiously. I felt her hand on the top of my head, then felt something soft slide through the part between my pigtails and down my neck. I sat scared stiff, thinking about the worms in my dreams.

"What is it?" I cried.

"It's a worm!" she cried and jumped up out of her chair.

"A worm in my hair?" I slapped the back of my neck where I felt something crawling. I screamed, reaching for it, snatching hair, skin, air, and finally found it. It was soft and slimy and long. I snatched it from my neck and flung it down on the table. There it was – a long slice of onion with gravy on it.

Lynette laughed so hard she held her stomach. "It's just a slice of onion!" she shouted, and then laughed even harder.

"You tricked me!" I shouted. I felt sick. I cried because I had thought Lynette cared about me. She knew I was scared of creepy crawling things and look how she treated me.

Out of all my sisters, why did Lynette want to hurt me so much? I thought. She's the one who told me, "Don't ever run from roaches 'cause you're bigger than them. Kill them or they'll get you." She even showed me how to step on them and wiggle my shoe to make sure the roach was dead. How could she tell me to be brave and then scare me herself?

With my fork I lifted the onion slice Lynette had pulled through my hair and placed it on the rim of my plate. I was so angry with my big sister that I lost my appetite. I dropped down in my chair, covered both eyes with my hands, and cried.

My big sister Beverly, who didn't talk much, yelled at Lynette, "That was a mean trick to play on a little girl!" Then she rushed over and took me by the hand and led me to the bathroom. She washed the gravy from the smashed onion out of my hair and off my neck and hands.

After I was cleaned up, I went to my room because I was too embarrassed to finish eating my dinner.

* * *

I think it was Beverly who once said, "History repeats itself." Well, I learned what that meant soon after the onion and gravy trick. I felt like a fraidy cat for real the next Sunday after Zenobia and I had gone to Mt. Nebo Baptist Church.

Zenobia had a tiny waist and big behind like Mama. She liked to hold her left arm up in the air like her wrist was broken while she carried her pocketbook on her arm. A lot of boys stared at her when we walked to church and three of them even followed her as we walked back home. On the way home, I was walking alongside her laughing because the boys whistled at her as she switched down the street. But she ignored them.

"Just pretend you don't hear them and they'll keep on whistling," she said with a smile.

I could tell that she was having fun getting all that attention. I giggled all the way home as the boys followed us, whistling, until we turned into our front yard.

I was still giggling when we reached our house. I followed Zenobia up the wooden steps to the side porch connecting our duplex with the neighbor's house. I stopped giggling the moment I noticed a tin tub almost full of blood.

"Oh, No! Mama done killed Daddy!" I shrieked and shrank back. I was too afraid to go inside.

"You don't know what you're talking about!" Zenobia shouted back as she turned and tried to pry my hands away from the banister. I was clenching the banister and screaming my head off.

My short and skinny Mama heard me outside scream-ing and rushed through the side screen door as Zenobia stood on the porch trying to pull me up the last step.

"Where's Daddy?" I cried as soon as I saw Mama.

"He's in the house," Mama said, looking puzzled.

"Davida panicked when she saw that tub of blood," Zenobia told Mama.

"David hit me so I cut him with the butcher knife," Mama said nonchalantly. "He ran outside to wash his arm in that tub of water. The blood turned all the water red. He's all right. Come and see for yourself."

Mama grabbed my hand and I reluctantly followed her inside. Sure enough, there was Daddy sitting on the living room sofa with the front of his right arm wrapped in gauze and white adhesive tape just below the elbow.

Daddy was always getting hurt, but he was still alive! I ran to sit on the sofa close to my daddy, and carefully examined the gauze and tape. I gently touched his arm.

"Does it hurt?" I whispered. I shuddered as I sensed Daddy's pain.

"A little, but I'll live," Daddy said softly. "Don't worry about me; I hurt worse than this when I went to live with my papa."

"Tell us about it in story time," I said while motioning for my brother and younger sisters to gather around. They ran and sat at Daddy's feet on the floor around the sofa so they could see his face as he told his story.

I placed my index finger over my lips and whispered, "Sh-h-h-h-h," to remind everybody that story time meant it was time to listen. I also knew it was time for me to calm down and stop letting people scare me.

***

I smiled as I thought about story time on Sunday afternoons with Daddy. "I'll never ever forget my daddy's stories," I whispered, as I sat up in the dark room and wrapped my arms around my knees. The sound of chirping crickets interrupted my thoughts. *It's too late at night and too early in the morning to be chasing hopping crickets around the living room,* I groaned. I closed my eyes and wished the crickets would hush, but they didn't.

CHAPTER 17

I GOT UP AND TIPTOED over to the corner of the bedroom to use the night pot. After I squatted down on the night pot and peed, I eased the lid back on the pot so the noise wouldn't wake up anybody. Then I went to lie down again. As I lay in the darkness my mind raced back to thoughts about the story Daddy told us that Sunday afternoon back in the duplex when I was five. That's the day when Mama cut his arm with the butcher knife. I'm sure that big knife scared my daddy even though he said it didn't. I shuddered at the thought of Mama slicing Daddy's arm like it was a loaf of bread.

"Daddy must have been telling me not to let little things scare me," I mumbled as I sat thinking about life in the duplex.

I remembered how Daddy paused before he spoke. He took two puffs of his Winston cigarette then smashed the tip of it in the ashtray to put the fire out. He blew out the smoke and then it was story time.

When Daddy began to tell his story, I felt special because somebody cared enough to take time to talk to us and answer questions about things that mattered. The room was so quiet you could hear a pin drop as I snuggled close to Daddy's hurt arm. It was a little bit like Christmas too as the smell of Mama's good cooking filled the living room. I felt so special to be able to sit on the sofa close to my Daddy as he began to talk in his low, deep voice.

Daddy said, "My life was full of nothing but work, work, and more work until one beautiful August morning, six days before my fifteenth birthday. I was a few miles down the road picking cotton with Skinny Wesley, so I got most of this story second-hand from other people."

"Aunt Nadine was busy hanging clothes on the wire clothesline with wooden clothes pins while my mama placed firewood 'neath the huge, dangling, black cast iron kettle, the one she boiled our white clothes in on wash day. As mama doused the firewood, she spilt kerosene on the hem of her long cotton frock. When she leaned forward to swipe the side of a king-sized matchbox, sparks hit that kerosene and set her dress on fire. She ran around in circles flailing her arms and screaming like a madwoman. Flames shot up to her face."

"Aunt Nadine saw the fire and yanked a green wool Army blanket off the clothesline. She raced her short, two-hundred-pound body over to save her little sister. Aunt Nadine moved to the left holding out the open blanket to get close enough to toss it over her, but my mama moved to the right. When Aunt Nadine moved to the right or ran straight ahead my mama twisted and turned away."

"Hold still! You fanning the flames!" Aunt Nadine yelled 'til she finally threw the blanket over her and pushed mama down to the ground. She rolled my mama around like she was a lump of flour dough on waxed paper. By the time Aunt Nadine had pulled the blanket off my mama's head, nobody could say for sure whether your grandma Susie burned or suffocated to death."

"Aunt Nadine kept crying, the whole time, 'Help us Lord! Oh Lordy, please help us!' Our long-time neighbor, Mister Herb, was patching a hole in the fence along his property line when he saw smoke coming from over at our place. At first he said he thought nothing of it until he heard screams and saw Nadine running around. He climbed over the fence and ran to help them but he was too late. I guess God just said it was time for my mama to come up to heaven to be with Him."

"I had swept the yard the day before with a bundle of sticks that left streaks in the dirt. When I came home and saw my mama's body lying still on top of ashes, I saw that her footprints and a blanket had flattened those streaks. I found Aunt Nadine sitting on the ground beside my mama's burnt body. She was crying and rocking back and forth crying, *'I'm sorry, Susie! I'm sorry, Susie!'* she moaned all day and all night long."

Daddy shook his head like he was real sad. I felt my nose drip and I reached up and wiped with the back of my hand. I sniffed a couple of times as Daddy continued telling us how his mama died.

"People from near and far gathered 'round and they all could tell Aunt Nadine was in bad shape. I tried to lift my auntie off the ground but she was too heavy, or I just didn't have the strength. So I sat down beside her and put my face in my hands. I sat there and cried too. I kept wondering if I could have saved my mama if I had been at home. I would have felt much worse if this had happened one of those days when I was out working in the fields when I should have been at school. It was bad enough that I wasn't at home to help my mama but I would have felt much worser if I was out playing hooky the day mama died and nobody could find me when she needed my help."

"Mister Herb and the church handled all my mama's funeral arrangements. Every day before the funeral, Herb's wife and other neighbors brought food to the house for Aunt Nadine and me. I was a pretty good cook myself but I didn't feel like cooking or doing much else. My auntie's mind was so messed up that she had trouble answering when I called her name. She couldn't feed herself and she didn't wash her stink behind."

Daddy said, "Our house used to be spick-and-span. But after my mama died, the house smelled like number one and number two, so I hated to go home after work."

"It was Mister Herb who managed to find Ma's distant cousin who agreed to live in our house to take care of Aunt Nadine. Herb also arranged for me to go live with my long-lost papa. Mister Herb said he'd run into papa in a grocery store in Orangeburg, a couple of years earlier, but he didn't mention it 'cause, as he put it, 'Susie and Nadine were gitting 'long just fine without Bubba Kincaid.' That's when Mister Herb learned that

Charlotte had become papa's wife number three, but he left her shortly after she gave birth to a son, a brother I never met. My papa was with Eunice by this time, his wife number four."

My brother, little sisters and I were glued to Daddy's every word.

Daddy kept talking, "Mister Herb took it upon himself to go tell papa and Eunice the news of my mama's tragic death and the fact that Nadine couldn't take care of me. Papa and Eunice agreed that I should leave Bamberg and move to Orangeburg to live with them and their seven children. Mister Herb convinced me that it was best to go live with my papa. He even drove me there three weeks after mama's death."

"At first I was excited about seeing my papa again after ten years of wondering where he'd gone and how he looked after he broke loose from Miss Charlotte's hair. I was shocked when the old chap told me, 'I've got twenty-one children by four different women so don't 'spect no special treatment.' I'd thought it would be great to be 'round my papa. I don't know why I thought he would be glad to see me and tell me how sorry he was that my mama died the way she did. But nope, he hadn't changed a bit in all them years. He had fights with Eunice just like he had with my mama. He just never walked out on her and her children. I guess he stayed 'cause he had gout and poor circulation in his legs."

"Eunice and her children made me feel welcome. But being the oldest child in the house meant I had to work harder than the rest. It didn't take long for me to make up my mind to grow up real fast so I could hurry up and get out of papa's house."

"Not one time did my papa ever mention why he walked out of my life without coming back. He never even wrote me a letter. He forgot all about me from the minute he walked out. I never had the courage to ask him about it neither. I always felt like I didn't belong in that house, even though Eunice made sure I had more than

my fair share of work to do around there. Before long, I
realized I was already a grown man."

Daddy looked straight at us and said, "Ya'll listen
to me. When I needed my papa he was nowhere 'round.
That's why I told ya'll, 'I will never leave my children'."

After daddy said that, I saw a lump in his throat jump
up and down and he choked on his words. He cleared
his throat like he was going to cry. It hurt me real bad to
watch him. I usually had lots of questions, but that day I
waited awhile before I said anything.

Everyone was quiet. Finally, I whispered, "Daddy,
why did Mama cut you today?"

"Well now, I raised my arm and your mama swung
at me in self-defense 'cause I made her mad," he replied.
"It was my fault." Then Daddy asked me, "What'd the
preacher talk about in church today?"

"He talked about a boy named David who killed a
giant with a rock and a slingshot," I said. Then I thought
about my daddy having the name David too. "Did your
parent's name you after the David in the Bible?"

Daddy laughed. He probably laughed because he
managed to make me think of something better than his
wounded arm. I got up and moved over to his other side
and leaned my head against his good arm. He said, "I
see preachers still tell the same ole stories they told back
when I was a boy. Yep, my mama wanted me to be strong
and of good courage like that David with the slingshot."

"Your mama got her wish," I said. "You are strong
and of good courage."

That was the truth because one thing I knew for sure,
my Daddy was strong and of good courage when it came
to whupping us with his leather strap. Sometimes he
beat my sisters so long and hard that Mama had to make
him stop.

As I listened to Daddy tell why his mama named
him David, all of a sudden I remembered one night
when Zenobia was 15. She climbed out of the bedroom
window to go with her friend to see a concert at the

Columbia Township Auditorium. She went but she got caught trying to sneak back in through our bedroom window. Daddy was waiting for her. He waited until she had climbed all the way inside the dark bedroom and then he turned on the light. He tore her behind up with his barber's razor strap.

Mama ran in and pleaded with him, "Stop, David, stop, before you break her legs! Can't you see she's bleeding?"

I think I felt every lick Zenobia got. I made up my mind that night that I was going to do my duty to keep that strap off my booty. Daddy was still talking about his name when Mama yelled, "Dinner's ready!"

I grabbed Daddy's good hand and escorted him to the kitchen table as I tried to put the sight of a tub of blood out of my mind. I had no idea that after dinner I would have a good reason to be scared of a whupping with Daddy's good hand.

* * *

I tossed and turned as I thought about the excitement in our house years ago when we all lived together with Mama and Daddy. I had seen and heard an awful lot of bad things.

CHAPTER 18

I ROLLED OVER and tried to go back to sleep but couldn't. Bad thoughts kept flooding my mind. I continued thinking about what happened on the evening Mama cut Daddy's arm.

After the trouble in our house, peace came at the dinner table. All I heard was the clanging sound of forks connecting with plates and teeth as we gobbled Mama's delicious macaroni and cheese, string beans and fried pork chops. One cut arm didn't stop my daddy from enjoying his meal. Daddy picked up his pork chop by the bone with his left hand and gnawed at it with his pearly white teeth. Nobody would have guessed there had been a big fight in our house just a few hours ago.

As a matter of fact, I really couldn't tell which one Mama and Daddy liked best, fighting or making up. They seemed to understand each other. I'm the one who couldn't understand why they kept fighting.

After dinner, Lynette and I put our dirty plates in the sink and walked toward the front door at the same time. It was Beverly's turn to wash dishes so we were free to leave the kitchen. I gently tugged at Lynette's arm and she turned and leaned down so I could whisper in her ear. I put both my hands around her ear and whispered, "How can Daddy act like nothing bad happened to him today?"

She laughed and whispered in my ear, "Husbands and wives don't have to have a reason to get on each other's nerves."

As soon as I got outside Lynette disappeared from sight as I skipped across our big front yard to see if my best friend Lisa could come outside and play. Lisa, one year older than I was, lived on the second floor of her parent's funeral home. I sang, "Skip, skip, skip to my Lou" while thinking about the fun games we played together like jacks, hopscotch, rick-rack, school, and house with dressed up doll babies or paper dolls made out of brown paper bags. I thought about jumping rope, shooting marbles, climbing a tree, or playing detective. Detective was a game we made up ourselves for the times when we inspected dead bodies at Foster's Funeral Home to try to guess how the person died.

I was thinking that today, maybe Lisa and I could join other children in a game of *Simon Says, Red Light/ Green Light, Tisket-a-Tasket, Spin the Bottle,* or *Little Sally Walker.*

Suddenly I spotted my chubby friend Lisa running toward me as the sun was going down that warm summer evening.

"Boy am I glad to see you!" Lisa cried. She was breathing real hard like a dog had been chasing her. It was either that or something else had scared her.

"What's wrong with you?" I asked. "Did you see a ghost?"

"C'mon, let me show you the new body that just came in." She grabbed my hand and turned around. She began pulling me after her but I pulled in the opposite direction.

"Whoa! Wait! We've seen lots of dead bodies before," I said. "What's so different about this one?" Curiosity was bubbling inside my tummy by then because I'd never seen Lisa so excited about anything.

"It's a surprise!" she said. "We'll view the body then go across the street to get some candy." Lisa was the one who kept a dime or nickel on her. Whenever she bought Squirrel Nuts or Butter Logs or purple bubble gums she shared them with me. She knew I didn't have a penny to my name.

"Let me go and ask Mama first," I said as I twisted my skinny arm to break loose from her grip.

She knew my daddy was known for whupping us with the kind of leather strap barbers use to sharpen their razor.

"I'd better ask Mama so I won't get a whupping." I said. I tried to wring my arm out of her grip again but she had a strong hold on my wrist.

"No! Let's make it our little secret," Lisa whispered, even though nobody else was around. "I promise we'll come right back. I want you to see a man who was electrocuted. It looks like he had a lampshade on his head. Then we can go get some candy and come right back. Nobody will ever miss us."

"W-e-l-l, all right," I said. "But this had better be quick."

I was intrigued by the secret outing and curious about the lampshade on the dead man's head. She eased open the front door and I followed close behind her as she tiptoed down the hallway into what used to be the garage of the funeral home. She gently closed the door behind us and turned on the light. There lay a bald-headed man in a wooden box. Sure enough, I saw a black ring around the man's head.

"Oh, my gosh!" I whispered. "Look at that black ring around his head. It looks like somebody fried his head. What do you think caused it?"

"Uhhhh –," she said.

"That must have been so painful! Even a tiny little burn hurts me. Ugh! Ugh! I can't stand to look at this one. I'm getting out of here!" I turned to run out the door as Lisa held it open for me. She followed me out of the garage and closed the door behind us.

"See, I told you this one was different," she whispered. "It looks like streaks of lightning covered his bald head. Hey, let's go out this way."

The image of the dead man's scalp remained fresh in my mind as we sneaked out through a side door of Foster's funeral home. We ran past a parked ambulance and then darted across the street since there was not a car in sight.

From out of nowhere, a car careened down the hill as we neared the curb on the opposite side of the street. I heard the sound of screeching brakes. It seemed as though I heard people screaming, but they sounded far away. I opened my eyes to see what was happening and blinked a few times before I saw people hovering over me in a circle. Suddenly, I heard a loud voice, "Coming through!"

Two men pushed through the circle and knelt down beside me. I felt something hard under my back and that's when I realized that I was lying in the street. I opened my eyes as the men were poking different parts of my body. The next thing I knew, I was gazing up at the top floors of the Columbia Hospital. I heard a motor running and then the siren of an ambulance as it sped away with a flashing red light hitting the ground. I heard running footsteps just moments before I felt myself being lifted onto a wobbly bed with wheels. I felt myself being pushed around in a jerky motion. I couldn't move.

Instantly, I got scared that I would end up in a wooden box like the man I had just seen at Foster's Funeral home. Then a greater fear gripped me as I thought about my daddy whupping me with that big leather strap for sneaking off with Lisa.

I knew I should have asked Mama if I could go, I cried silently. I felt extremely tired and sleepy. I felt like I was drifting away on soft white clouds where none of my problems mattered. I didn't think another thought and I didn't hear another sound for a long time.

* * *

It seemed like I had just fallen asleep when I heard gospel music coming from the radio. I opened my eyes and saw daylight. It was time to get up and get ready for school even though I felt like I hadn't been to sleep at all.

CHAPTER 19

I WAS STILL SLEEPY as I ran up the hill to the school bus stop. After I sat down next to a window on the third seat, I closed my eyes to try to blot out the noisy chatter from the back seats as the school bus rolled along. In my mind, I tried to imagine myself sleeping the whole day on that Monday after a car hit me while Lisa and I were running across the street.

"I could use some of that sleep right now," I murmured. I was thinking, I guess I'll never know what happened on that Monday when I slept all day and all night like Rip Van Winkle. It's funny how life goes on when someone is no longer around.

Mama showed up at the hospital around noon on Tuesday and the nurse, in her southern drawl, gave her strict instructions.

"Your little girl is to be on complete bed rest for the next ten days," she said. "Make her lie flat on her back and don't let her lift a thing. The doctor says she'll probably have arthritis in her back, so he wants her to see a chiropractor."

I was too nervous about getting a whupping from Daddy to be worried about what the nurse was telling Mama. Mama turned toward me when the nurse finished talking.

"You must have an angel watching over you," Mama said, while taking my tank top and pair of shorts out of a brown paper bag. "You could've been killed."

"I'm sorry, Mama," I said.

Mama helped me change out of my hospital gown and put on the clean clothes she had brought for me. She took me by the hand and we walked through the hospital's big green double doors beneath the EXIT sign. I could see Foster's Funeral Home the moment we stepped into the sunshine. I smelled the fresh cut grass as the gardener pushed the lawnmower. Pretty flowers lined the sidewalk in front of the Columbia Hospital. It seemed odd that Mama didn't fuss at all about my going off without asking her permission. In fact, Mama said little or nothing as we walked hand-in-hand down the sidewalk toward our house, next door to Foster's Funeral Home.

As soon as we got home, Mama set up a rollaway bed in the living room just for me. She helped me put on my Wonder Woman pajamas before I lay down. From my bed near the front door I could see everybody who came in and went out, and they could see me too.

That day, my family began nursing me back to health by feeding me hot soup, speaking kind words to me, and gently rubbing me with liniment mixed with Johnson's Baby Oil. It felt so soothing, especially with everybody making me feel that they were glad to have me back home.

If this is love, then I don't ever want to get well, I thought.

After a few days, I felt guilty because I really enjoyed all the attention. That was unusual because in our house the newest baby always got the most attention. I started thinking a lot about Lisa and what she had called 'our little secret' when we slipped across the street. Secret? Now everybody in downtown Columbia must know that a car hit me. I think all the neighbors showed up to watch the ambulance pick me up out of the street. Why did I believe I could slip away and not be missed? I knew perfectly well how bad Daddy beat Zenobia when she sneaked out and got caught climbing back in through the window. I must have been crazy! Everybody knows parents have eyes in the back of their heads.

Every day I lay there in that rollaway bed wondering when I was going to get my whupping. Daddy was nice to me and he never mentioned a whupping. I was sure he was just waiting until I could stand up again.

On Tuesday, one week after I left the hospital, Mama put me in our little red wagon and pulled me up the sidewalk to see a chiropractor like the doctor at the hospital told her to do. I felt plenty jerked around before we even reached the doctor's office just a block away. The chiropractor jerked me around even more but that wasn't the same as a whupping.

"Come on in, Mrs. Kincaid," Dr. Youngblood said.

Mama grabbed my hand and I followed her into the doctor's office where I saw lots of big pictures of human bodies made out of bones hanging on the wall. Mama let go of my hand and then she sat down in a chair.

"I need you to climb up on my table," the white-haired doctor said.

As Mama watched, I climbed on the step and sat down on a bed with a big sheet of white paper on it. I wasn't scared one bit. As soon as I got on the table, Dr. Youngblood laid both of his big, cold hands on my head.

"This will only hurt you for just a minute," he said. "Relax."

After I sat still for a moment, I heard popping sounds coming from my neck as the doctor suddenly twisted my head from side to side. He pushed hard on my body and jerked it all around. Mama watched him beat me all up and she didn't say a word. My bones made sounds like crackling lightning and I burst out laughing. He hurt me for a minute but then I felt better. It seemed like the doctor was playing a game with me.

"There," he said when he finished. "You won't be so stiff any more."

At the dinner table that night, Mama told everybody about our trip to the chiropractor.

"Davida just laughed and laughed every time that doctor jerked her around." Mama snapped her head between her two hands to show everybody how the chiropractor had jerked my head.

They laughed hard. I tried to laugh too but I felt kind of sore.

During my second visit, I heard the chiropractor talking to Mama.

"Your child will always have trouble with her back," Dr. Youngblood said.

When I heard what the doctor said, I decided to play sick a few days longer. When no one was watching me in the living room, I secretly sat up in bed just to make sure my back was okay. When others were present, I lay flat on my back, stiff as a board.

One day Lisa hobbled through the door using a crutch with her right leg in a cast. As soon as she saw me lying perfectly still, she burst out crying and had snot dripping from her nose. I knew right then that I had to tell her my secret.

I motioned with my index finger for her to come closer so I could whisper in her ear.

She sat down beside me on the edge of my rollaway bed and leaned her head over close to my head.

"I'm all right but I'm going to lie here as long as I can to keep Daddy from whupping me," I whispered in Lisa's ear.

She stared at me for a moment and then she giggled. "I guess we both learned to ask permission from now on," she said. "Then we won't have to feel guilty."

Three days later, I got tired of lying flat on my back all day and night so I got up and began to walk again. Besides, I wasn't getting as much attention as I did at first. I guess it's because I took too long to get well.

"You made a liar out of that doctor at the hospital!" Mama shouted as soon as she saw me walking toward the kitchen. "He said you might never walk again."

"Is Daddy going to whup me now?" I asked.

"David won't whup you," Mama said. "You already got your whupping when that car hit you. A drunk soldier from Fort Jackson was driving too fast and hit you and Lisa. Lisa was only knocked down 'cause she was out in front. You were pinned beneath the car and dragged a ways before the driver stopped the car."

"No wonder I saw the hospital when I opened my eyes!" I said.

"Only God kept you alive," Mama said.

"I'm sorry, Mama!" I cried with tears streaming down my cheeks as I wrapped my arms around Mama's waist. I buried my face in her chest, and sobbed, and sobbed, and sobbed.

"Let this be a good lesson for you," Mama said as she patted my back. "Children have no business crossing the street by themselves."

"I promise I'll be good from now on so nothing bad will happen to me," I said.

* * *

The next week I was sitting on the front steps with Harry. We were busy separating the cat eye marbles from all the others in a pail when I heard Daddy and Mama say something about "moving." I started listening closely as I held up a cat eye marble and took a closer look at it.

"My boss man said he sold the duplex to Foster's Funeral Home so they can expand," Daddy said. "I don't know where we gonna move to with all these children, but we gotta move."

"We can move to Marshall Village where my brother lives," Mama said. "I'll let Clyde know we looking to move pretty soon and maybe he can take us to see the place."

"I trust you to take care that business then," Daddy said. "You better start looking soon."

I sighed, thinking about all the babies who had been born during the years we lived in our downtown duplex. Even though she never looked pregnant, Mama had a new baby almost every year. Mama had Vera, who looked just like Daddy. Next came April, who always got lots of beautiful dresses from Mr. Henderson who lived in the house across the street facing ours. After the birth of our newest baby sister, Gladys, Mama let her stay at Grandma Cox's house for a long time before she brought her home. I was surprised to see how a baby girl could look just like a grown man. Gladys was the spitting image of Mr. Walter whose broad smile and pearly white teeth were etched in my memory. I'll never forget the way he was always smiling and staring into Mama's eyes.

On Saturday morning, Uncle Clyde brought three of his children with him when he came to take Mama to look at apartments in Marshall Village. Daddy couldn't go because he had to go to work. Mama got inside the pickup and all the children hopped on the back.

Uncle Clyde drove his truck like a torpedo trying to sink a submarine. I glanced down and saw my little sisters laughing as they were being tossed from one side of the truck to the other. Their arms were locked at the elbow as though they were clinging to each other for dear life.

Uncle Clyde got a kick out of catching a green light just before it turned red. He liked to laugh and cheer like he had won an Olympic gold medal when he caught a green light. The truck squealed and seemed to lean on two wheels as Uncle Clyde caught a light on Harden Street.

Suddenly, I lost my grip on the metal headboard as the pickup made a sharp left turn while I was looking down at the children rolling around. Before I realized it, I was soaring over the side of the truck.

"Dang! I'm flying! Oh, help me Jesus!" I yelled.

"Thump!" My body hit the pavement and I landed in the middle of the intersection near Benedict College and Allen University. The light turned green as I rolled along the middle of the street toward three lanes of oncoming traffic.

If the cars roll over me, I'll be okay as long as the tires don't squish me, I thought. None of the cars in the three lanes moved. I stopped rolling, jumped up, and started chasing Uncle Clyde's truck. I thought of myself getting hit by a car again, and lying in the street. I glanced over my shoulder and saw cars in all three lanes following me in slow motion.

"I've got to outrun them," I said, as I ran at full throttle down the center lane. "Jesus, please let the drivers see me!"

I could see my cousins banging on the truck's small rear window trying to get Uncle Clyde's attention. I ran faster. Finally, Uncle Clyde stopped in the center lane before he reached the next traffic light. He got out and stood beside the truck holding his door open. When I reached the back he scooped me up and dumped me in the truck bed on the driver's side.

"I can tell you didn't break nothing the way you were galloping," he said half grinning. "Stay down on the floor!" Then he got back inside, slammed his door shut, and drove away.

I lay in the bed of the truck sobbing, and rubbing my stinging, scraped up arms and legs, trying to catch my breath. All the children watched me as they held on to each other or the bottom of the headboard. I cried all the way to Uncle Clyde's house. I cried because I could have been hit by a car again, but I wasn't. I also cried because I could've been left all alone in that big street if my brother and cousins hadn't made Uncle Clyde wait for me. My nose was bleeding. I felt real bad but then I felt good. I was hurting all over but not as bad as when I got hit by a car.

Uncle Clyde drove to the back of his apartment and dropped all the children off. He lifted me off the back onto my feet. Then he drove Mama over to the Marshall Village rent office so they could catch it open before it closed at noon.

My cousin Homer grabbed my hand and walked with me. As soon as we got inside he told Aunt Judy, "Davida went flying off the back of the truck when Daddy turned the corner real fast. I lost my grip too but I hurried up and caught hold again."

"Aren't grownups supposed to watch out for children?" I asked. "Everybody ought to be strapped down so they can't fly off a truck. How can we know to hold on if we're in the back and can't see the light. What if we're sleeping? It's not my fault Uncle Clyde turned the corner like that."

"I know Clyde drives wild like that," Aunt Judy said. "I tell him 'bout it all the time. I see you scraped your nose. Sit down and let me fix you up."

She reached in the cabinet and pulled out a shoebox and brought it to the chair where I was sitting. I could see the tube of ointment, Q-Tips, Band-Aids, cotton balls and all the same things Mama kept in a shoebox at home. Seeing that box made me feel like I was going to get fixed up in a short time.

Aunt Judy screwed the stopper off a tiny glass bottle of Iodine and squeezed drops of red liquid on my scrapes.

"OUCH!" I screamed as I tried to push her hand away.

"It'll only sting for a minute," Aunt Judy said. "After the sting goes away this stuff will keep those nasty scrapes from getting infected."

"OUCH!" I cried every time she worked on a new scrape. She gently dabbed ointment on my scraped nose with the white cotton Q-Tip. Last of all, she opened a bottle of Tiger Balm liniment and the strong smell of medicine filled the air. I coughed a few times as she rubbed my back and chest and all over my body. I felt like a big greasy and smelly ball by the time she finished.

"It's a miracle you didn't get hit by a car or break any bones falling in the street like that," Aunt Judy said. "Jesus protected you, child! Don't you ever forget it! You better thank him!"

"Thank you Jesus!" I said.

"Why did something bad happen to me even when I tried to do the right thing?" I asked myself. Then I silently asked Jesus, "What did I do wrong this time?"

"What's that smell?" Uncle Clyde shouted as soon as he walked through the door behind Mama.

"You know that's liniment!" Mama said. She took one look at me and said, "Seems like trouble follows Davida ev'rywhere she goes."

I opened my mouth to say it wasn't my fault this time, but Aunt Judy started talking.

"Well, did ya'll get the 'partment?" she said.

"We sure did," Mama said. "We got number 7-A, right 'cross from you. Ya'll gonna have new neighbors by the end of the next month."

"Welcome," Aunt Judy said. "The children'll love it here."

* * *

On the day we moved to Marshall Village that summer, as soon as Uncle Clyde backed his red pickup all the way up to the front porch of our duplex, Mama hurried down the steps with baby Gladys in her arms before he turned off the engine.

"Take me and the children over there first, then come back for the furniture," Mama said. Then she climbed into the front seat and put Gladys on her lap.

I stood beside the truck talking to Lisa while Harry, Vera, and April climbed on the back.

Zenobia, Lynette, and Beverly stayed at the house with Daddy to move furniture and stack boxes on the front porch.

"I think moving means I'll never see you again," I tearfully told Lisa. "I heard Daddy say we had to move so your parents' funeral home can have more room. They're going to tear down our duplex. That means I'll never see you or our house again."

"I don't know anything about my parents buying your house," she said. "All I know is, I'm going to miss you. You're my bestest friend in the whole wide world."

We hugged each other and cried together. It hurt because our parents didn't tell us about things that affected us. Don't grownups know that children have feelings too? I thought, as I climbed on board and sat down on back of the pickup.

"Davida, you watch out for your little sisters since you're the oldest one back there," Mama said. "Your daddy and big sisters gonna come later on with the furniture so y'all won't be in the way."

"Bye-bye," everybody," Lisa hollered as Uncle Clyde pulled out of the dirt driveway.

"Bye-bye! So long! See you later, alligator!" my older sisters shouted from the front porch.

"After while, crocodile," Daddy shouted and laughed.

I waved goodbye with one hand and gripped the bottom of the headboard with the other as I sat on the floor of the pickup along with my little sisters and brother.

"Uncle Clyde won't kill me on this moving adventure!" I mumbled.

My stomach started churning with a mix of sadness and gladness. I was eager to see what Marshall Village had in store for me. All kinds of thoughts crossed my mind as Uncle Clyde's pickup rattled along busy Harden Street. "Moving seems like searching for a prize in a box of Cracker Jacks," I mumbled. "You know the prize is in there somewhere but you have to dig to find it, or shake up the box to let it fall to the top, or empty the Cracker Jacks out to find it." I hope I get a fun surprise, I thought. Something I can't even imagine.

"Hmmmm... Now what could that be?" I asked myself.

Maybe everybody in my family will make friends with lots of people and Mama will find some lady friends who stay at home and take care of their babies too. Maybe I'll find lots of good places to play hide and seek. Lots of children were playing all over the grass and sidewalk when we went to Uncle Clyde's house. Maybe my prize will be to make friends with lots of children my age. If Harry has some boys to play with, then we'll all be happy. It will be a great prize if Mama and Daddy don't fight anymore. Maybe the city police will tell Daddy he can't whup us with his strap anymore in those crowded buildings where people can hear you talking through the walls. No more whuppings would be the best prize ever!

As the pickup rattled along toward Marshall Village, I kept trying to picture living in another house and what would happen to our old house.

"I don't know what the hidden prize is yet, but I just FEEL like something good is coming out of this move!" The words slid off my tongue louder than I intended to say.

"Yeah, Sis! I think you're right," Harry said.

I giggled at Harry's words. I must have been thinking aloud. All of the old thoughts twisted and turned in my brain. Then all the hurt and sadness about my old house turned into something like a word called *happiness*. I could feel it everywhere, in the air, in my pea green shorts and flowered halter top, in my heart, pounding— "New! New! New!"

I held on tighter and smiled when Uncle Clyde's truck turned into Marshall Village.

* * *

I glanced out the window when the school bus came to a screeching halt. I had completely forgotten that I was on my way to school.

CHAPTER 20

THE LONG BUS RIDE to and from school every day gave me plenty of time to think, so that's just what I did while riding home that afternoon. I closed my eyes and pictured in my mind our move from the duplex in downtown Columbia to our apartment in Marshall Village.

I'll never forget that hot summer day when we arrived in Marshall Village. It was before I started the first grade. I ran from room to room enthusiastically examining our new home. I strutted across the living room that I knew would turn into a bedroom at night. I ran my hand along the shiny ceramic countertops in the kitchen that had a two-door icebox and an electric range already in place. When I opened the door to the icebox and electric range, I imagined seeing plenty of food in the empty icebox and hot sugar biscuits baking in the cold oven. I tested the faucets above the kitchen sink. The hot and cold water worked just fine. I made sure to check out everything in the kitchen, even the empty pantry.

As I left the kitchen, I slid my hand along the concrete walls as I passed through the little hallway on my way to the two empty bedrooms. "When Daddy puts our bunk beds in here they'll cover up most of these walls, " I mumbled as I stared at the bare bedroom walls. "There's not much to see here."

Next I went to check out the bathroom at the end of the little hallway across from a big empty closet. "I'm going to like taking a warm bath with baby oil and Ivory soap in this deep bathtub," I thought as I turned on the hot and cold faucets and let a little water run through my fingers. I turned off the water and wiped my hand on the side of my pea green shorts. The wet fingerprints left spots on my shorts. I left the bathroom and walked to the back door then turned around and tiptoed across the kitchen and living room. I counted aloud from one to forty-four as I stepped on square black tiles with tiny white polka dots in them until I reached the front door. I looked back across the empty room and nodded my head.

"This is going to be all right!" I said.

When I finished exploring the inside of our new apartment it was time to explore the outside. I went out the front door and sat down with my hands beneath my buns to keep the hot concrete stoop from burning me. I felt like I was on a great adventure. I got excited when I looked to my right and saw rows of apartment buildings and hundreds of children playing outdoors.

As I sat down on the stoop I noticed two girls about my age playing hopscotch in front of the end apartment in the next building. As I watched them playing, one of the girls stared at me for a moment and then hopped right out of boxes 7 and 8 and started walking in my direction. The Carolina sun cast a huge shadow on the girl's two thick pigtails that were sticking up like cow's horns. I fought hard to keep from laughing as I watched her coming my way with her larger-than-life shadow with horns, walking beside her. She kept her eyes on me while the other girl ran to catch up with her.

"Wait, I'm coming too!" the other girl yelled.

"Hey! I'm Mary Jane and this is my friend, Glendora," she boldly announced. "Do you like to play Jacks?" She reached in the pocket of her blue jean shorts and pulled out a plastic bag of jackstones and a new red rubber ball.

"Yeah!" I answered. "I'm Davida. We just moved here from downtown."

"Can you play right now?" she asked.

"Yeah," I said. "I'm just waiting for my daddy and big sisters to come with the furniture and boxes."

Mary Jane sat down across from me on the stoop and we played our first game of Jacks. The concrete didn't seem so hot anymore when I removed my hands and sat down on the stoop. Mary Jane sat down beside me and

Glendora stood watching while the two of us played our first game of jacks. Mary Jane was good, but I was better. She told me everything she knew about Marshall Village, her only home for all six years of her life.

Then, I told her about my life in downtown Columbia. She already knew everyone our age who lived in Marshall Village so she and Glendora promised to help me get to know them too.

These new friends will keep me from missing my best friend Lisa, I thought.

That same day after I beat her in our first game of jacks, Mary Jane asked me, "Do you want us to be best friends?"

"Yeah," I said. "I like living here already. It will be so much fun having wide open fields to run in and sidewalks where we can play hopscotch and dodge ball."

"Let's all swear to be best friends," Mary Jane said.

Mary Jane, Glendora and I each licked the tip of our index finger then touched our forehead, our belly button and the tips of our shoulders as we said all together, "I cross my heart and hope to die." That sealed our best friendship from that moment on.

My new friend Mary Jane and I had two things in common. First, she liked to play jacks as much as I did. Second, her mama had lots of children too. The only difference between us was that Mary Jane had never seen her daddy and didn't even know his name.

"Gosh, I feel special because my daddy lives with us," I said. "He'll be coming home anytime now."

"I live with my mama and daddy," Glendora said.

"Wow! You're the only child?" I stared at her for a moment. "You are so lucky."

"Lemme show you around," Mary Jane said.

"Wait! I've got to ask my mama," I said. I pressed my face against the screen door and yelled, "Mama, can I go walking with my new friends?"

"Go on," Mama yelled back from the kitchen. "There's nothing we can do right now anyhow."

Glendora and I followed Mary Jane when she headed straight to the back of our building on a walking tour of Marshall Village. I saw rows of faded blue apartments connected with black tar roofs. Behind the buildings was a big and scary place with lots of tall trees. The wooded area was shaped like a giant bowl right in the middle of Marshall Village. We stood along the edge of the woods talking as Mary Jane pointed to a muddy dirt path that ran from the street behind Building Number Seven where we lived in 7-A, to the opposite side of the wooded-area behind Building Number Eight where Uncle Clyde lived.

"Down there gives me the creeps!" Mary Jane said while pointing at the path. She seemed scared to look at the woods. She shook her head and said, "I never go through there. I take the long way around on the sidewalk."

I glanced around and saw Uncle Clyde backing his truck up to our back stoop. It was time for me to go home.

"I have to go home now because my daddy is here. But I'll see you later," I said. I turned and ran back to our apartment eager to tell everybody about my new friends.

Daddy and Uncle Clyde were already carrying in the sofa by the time I got home.

* * *

After Uncle Clyde and Daddy left for the second load, I went out on the back stoop and stared at the wooded area. The place gave me the creeps too, so I gave it a nickname.

"I'll call it Creepy Crater," I said to myself.

I made up my mind to use the sidewalk like Mary Jane to get to the other side where Uncle Clyde lived in 8-C. But one day Harry persuaded me to take the shortcut through Creepy Crater because Mama told us to run over to 8-C and borrow a cup of sugar from Aunt Judy.

"There's nothing to be afraid of, Sis," Harry said. "I'll be with you."

"All right. But you'd better not leave me," I said. I followed close behind him as he ran down the hill on the path through Creepy Crater.

I squinted to keep spider webs out of my eyes because I saw them all over the place as I ran real fast to keep up with Harry. I hollered real loud to scare away any dangerous thing until I was safely out of the woods. Spiders taught me that they don't care about the path people make through the woods. They just build their webs wherever they want to, especially across the path. After we got the cup of sugar and ran back home through Creepy Crater, I couldn't believe the spiders had built their web right back in the same spot where we had just knocked it down.

"Dumb critters!" I yelled, while flailing my arms as I ran to keep up with Harry on the way back home. That one time through the woods to borrow a cup of sugar was enough to convince me to stay out of Creepy Crater.

* * *

There was so much to see in Marshall Village that I soon forgot about our downtown duplex. I enjoyed watching big children do wheelies on bicycles on the narrow asphalt street out back. That's where I first saw thirteen-year-old Junior, the boy who lived next door in the end apartment, riding his bicycle with outstretched arms.

"Look Ma, no hands!" he yelled as he whizzed past one afternoon while Mary Jane and I were sitting on the back stoop playing jacks.

Mary Jane laughed and said, "It sure would be funny if he falls off his bicycle. Then he'd yell, 'Look Ma, no teeth!'"

We both laughed. I could just see Junior with two chipped front teeth.

"That's a bad thought," I said as we continued playing jacks. "When I get a bicycle, I'll stick to playing it safe by putting both hands on the handlebars."

The street behind our apartment had lots of traffic other than bicycles. The iceman drove through Marshall Village twice a week selling twenty-five pound blocks of ice for twenty-five cents each. The vegetable man came through once a week selling fresh produce that he weighed on a rusty scale that dangled from the makeshift roof of his dilapidated pickup truck. The milkman delivered two quart-sized bottles of fresh milk to our back stoop every morning. A paperboy road his bike by and tossed *The State* newspaper on the stoop before daybreak every morning.

We didn't have a car. But anytime we wanted to go somewhere all we had to do was walk up the hill to Barnwell Street and catch the city bus. Marshall Village Elementary School was at the top of the hill across the street from Cooper's Corner Store and Holy Cross Church. Next to Cooper's Corner Store there was a shoe repair shop, then a dry cleaning shop, a Laundromat, and the barbershop where Daddy took my brother Harry with him every two weeks to get a haircut. On the end of the row of businesses was a beauty salon that I never went to.

Mama straightened our hair with a hot-comb that burned the neck of all the girls in my family more times than I can remember. She always told me to sit still so she could press "my kitchen," the nappy hair on the back of my neck. Even when I froze up and didn't even breathe, she still burned me. I hated getting my hair straightened with a hot comb. If God wanted us to have straight hair he could have given it to us just like he gave it to other people, I thought. I didn't understand why we had to put heat on our scalp.

Mama got a Singer sewing machine and made most of our clothes. She bought a big bolt of fabric and made something for all of us, including Harry – her only boy. She made some pretty clothes by laying the fabric out on a fragile paper pattern and using stickpins to hold the pieces in place. Then she cut out the pieces with pinking shears so they looked like a jigsaw puzzle. I liked the clothes Mama made much better than the ones she bought for us.

"Mama I love living here in Marshall Village," I said one day as I watched her stitching a piece of cloth while the sewing machine whirred. "We have everything we need. Let's stay here all the time."

"We'll see," Mama said. "We'll see how long we stay here is all I can say."

After dinner that night Daddy mumbled something that sounded like, "I'll be back later."

He walked out the back door. I ran to the door, pulled back the café curtain, and watched him walk real fast across the street and then go down into the path in Creepy Crater. When I turned away from the windowpane in the kitchen door, I saw Mama closing the front door. Through the big picture window, I saw my skinny Mama's big behind switching up the hill in front of our house.

"Living here is great!" I shouted as I watched Mama switch out of sight at the top of the hill. "Everybody in our family has some new friends, even Mama and Daddy!"

"Ha! Ha!" Zenobia laughed. "That's what you think because you don't know any better! Daddy went to visit Miss Annie Mae and Mama's gone to see Mr. Fred. Everybody in the village knows that. Mama wasn't joking when she said, 'Two can play this game'."

Suddenly, Zenobia stuck her finger right between my eyes and said, "You'd better not mention what I just said or you'll be in B-I-G trouble. Do you hear me, Davida?"

I nodded 'yes,' several times as Lynette and Beverly watched. They were laughing at me. They knew I was scared of Zenobia. They made me wish I had never opened my mouth to tell anybody how much I liked living in Marshall Village. No matter what Zenobia said, I still loved my new home.

* * *

With textbooks in my arms, I slowly descended the school bus steps wondering what this Friday afternoon had in store for me. The flashback of watching Mama climb up the hill to visit Mr. Fred made me feel sick to my stomach. That drunk man was not the prize I had expected to find in Marshall Village.

I kicked a few rocks as I poked along toward our country house. I was still thinking about the exciting life I had found, and then left behind, in Marshall Village. I looked up at the blue sky and prayed, "God, please don't let Mr. Fred show up tonight."

CHAPTER QUESTIONS
FOR PERSONAL REFLECTION

1. How did you learn about marriage and divorce?
2. What helps a child adjust to a drastic change in family life?
3. How can a marriage survive betrayal?
4. How can a child avoid imitating a parent's bad example?
5. What are the duties of the eldest child?
6. How can kindness trigger shame?
7. What are some responsibilities children should not have?
8. What family secrets are too shameful to discuss?
9. Why is moving an emotional experience?
10. What causes a child to thrive?
11. Who knows what's best for you?
12. How do you respond to a new revelation?
13. What are some good substitutes for your daddy or mama?
14. Why is mental illness often viewed as shameful?
15. Why do some husbands and wives give up on their marriage?
16. How can a child become an emotional wreck?
17. How can a person invite suffering?
18. How do you show people that you care for them?
19. What shameful experiences do you need to let go of today?
20. Who are the friends who will encourage you after you let go of the garbage in your life?

ABOUT THE AUTHOR

GLORIA SHELL MITCHELL earned both a B.S. in Business Administration and Master of Accountancy from the University of South Carolina. She earned her Master of Arts in Christian Education at Golden Gate Baptist Theological Seminary, CLAD teaching credential from CSU, Dominquez Hills, and Doctor of Ministry in Spiritual Formation from Azusa Pacific University.

For more than thirty years she has been involved in youth ministry as well as teaching at the secondary, community college and university levels. As an ordained minister of the gospel, she is passionate about three Fs: sharing her faith, controlling finances and strengthening families. Since 1995 she has produced the weekly radio broadcast, *Good News For You,* on KTYM AM 1460, Inglewood, CA. As a Certified Public Accountant she served as the first African American and first female controller of Meharry Medical College. She is an adjunct mathematics instructor, divorce group facilitator, conference organizer and speaker, Bible teacher and chaplain. She is founder and executive director of JOY Youth Services, Inc., a nonprofit that advocates a holistic approach to educating youth.

Much of Dr. Mitchell's research in the area of divorce is included in her dissertation, *Compassionately Addressing Divorce: A Redemptive Model of Ministry to Divorced Christian Leaders.* She is the mother of two daughters, Richette and Joy, and resides in Los Angeles, CA.